CIRCLE ♥ loves PI

3.1415926535 846264338
8841971693993 209749445
640628620899862 825342117
4808651 230664 384460955
725359 284811 502841027
110555964622949 930381964
756659334461284 823378678
20190914564856 503486104
82133936073 73724587
5588174 82925409
678925 0548820

A Pi Day Story by
Vea Lewis

Hi Kids!

It's ME, everyone's favorite shape,

CIRCLE!

Did you know
that all of my friends
are easy to measure?

Especially, my friend Square.

But, not me.

I don't have sides that
are easy to measure with
a ruler. I have one **BIG** side
that goes all the way around.

Look at Square standing there!

All you have to do is put it next to him and see!

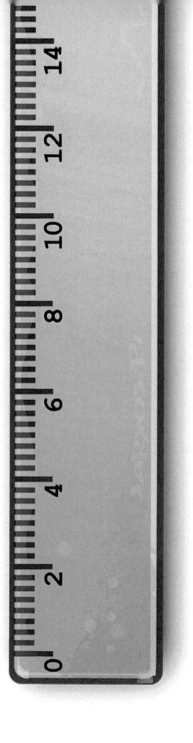

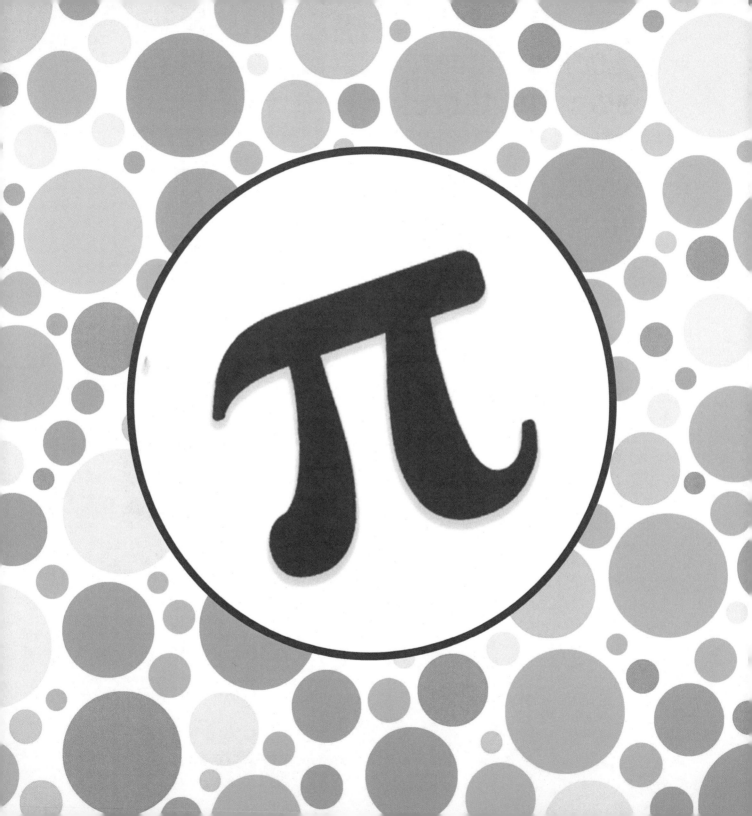

That's why I LOVE Pi

It's my simply stupendous,
frankly fantastic,
magically marvelous,
circle measuring secret weapon!

But what is Pi?

Pi is one of the two important numbers we have to measure circles. The **BEST** part of **PI** is that it's a **REALLY** long number.

3.141592653589793238
4626433832795028841 9
7169399375105820974 9
4459230781640628620
8998628034825342117
0679821480865132823
0664709384460955058
2231725359408128481 1
1745028410270193852 11

... it NEVER repeats itself
and it goes on and on FOREVER!

But all you have to remember is

3.14

What is the second number you ask?

Well, the second number is actually a

LETTER!

When we talk about circles the letter **R** stands for radius.

The radius is the distance from the center of a circle to the outer edge.

my radius

With pi and radius you can measure all kinds of circles!

Do you want to know how far an ant would walk if he walked on the edge of this cookie?

That's the CIRCUMFERENCE!

To find out, you need pi!

You can even use Pi to find the CIRCUMFERENCE

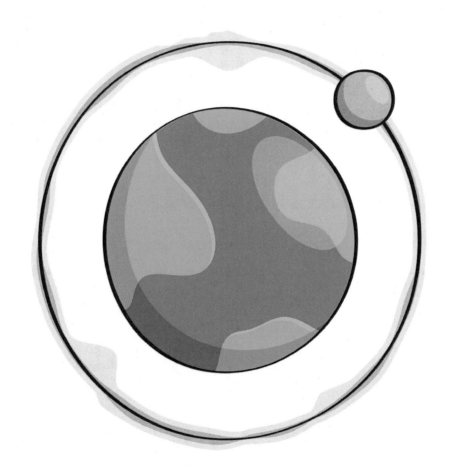

# of BIG circles, like the orbit of the Moon around the Earth!

Pi is AMAZING!

Do you want to know how much room you have on your pizza for toppings?

That's **AREA!**

Pi can help you figure that out, too.

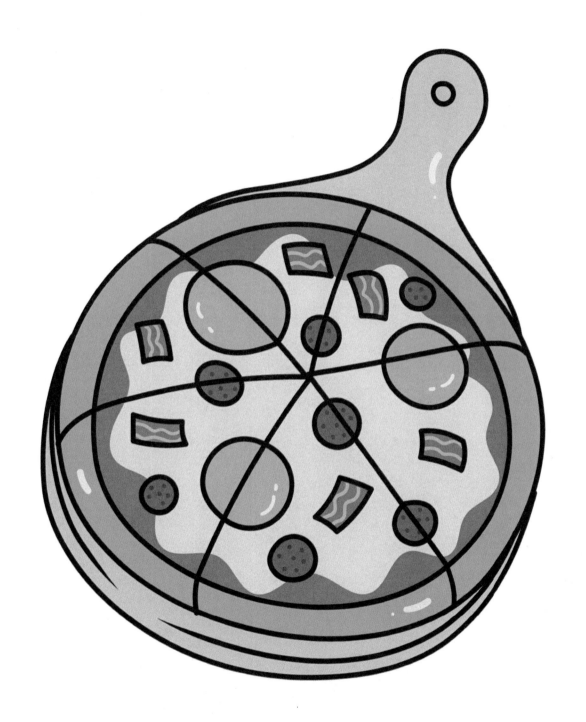

What about how much
milk you need to fill
a cylinder like a glass?

That's **VOLUME!**

You need Pi again!

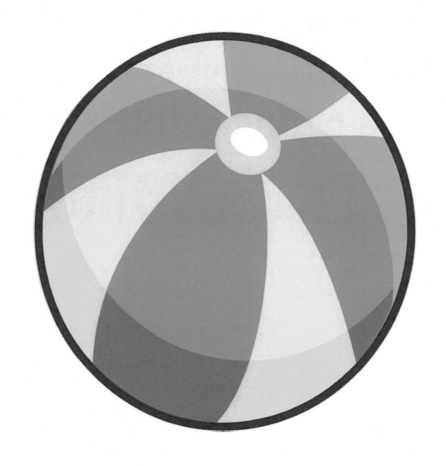

Are you filling a ball up with air?
If you measure how much you
need that is the **VOLUME**
of a **SPHERE!**

AND YOU NEED PI!

and of course,
you need Pi
to measure PIE!

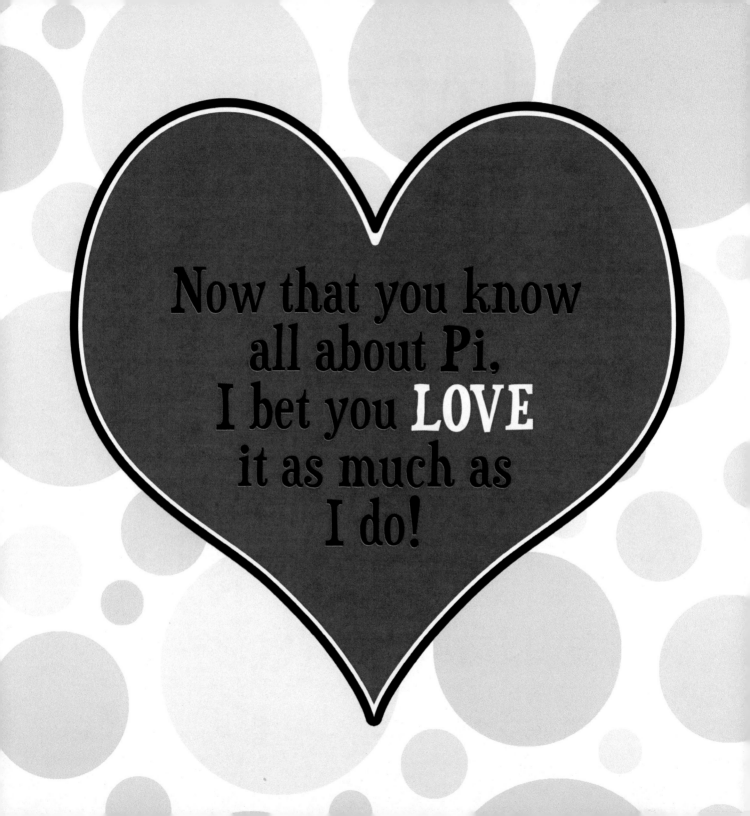

Do you need ideas to celebrate PI DAY? Try any of these ten activities!

1. Bake a pie and decorate it with the PI numbers.
2. Have a contest to see who can remember the most digits in Pi.
3. Draw some Pi puns. Ex: Chicken Pot Pi and Pi-rates.
4. Dress up in Pi clothes, you can even make your own!
5. Play the Pi card game. The rules are online and all you need is a deck of cards.
6. Measure the circumference of circles in your house or class.
7. Bake some Pi cookies to hand out to your friends.
8. Write all the words you can think of that start with Pi!
9. Watch Pi videos on Youtube! There is so much more for you to learn about Pi.
10. Visit VeaLewis.com for more FREE games and printables!

printed in the united states of america
first printing, 2022

seven monkeys publishing

THE DEFINITIVE

BLACKSTONE
OUTDOOR GAS GRIDDLE
Cookbook

Uncover the Secrets to Griddle Perfection with
Mouthwatering, Irresistible and Affordable
American Recipes | Perfect for Summer and
Year-Round Feasts

Alex & Jamie
Blake

Table of Content

Congratulations! You've Unlocked Blackstone Griddle Mastery!

Welcome to the world of effortless grilling, sizzling breakfasts, and endless culinary possibilities! This guide to Blackstone Griddle cooking isn't just a collection of recipes – it's your passport to a whole new level of outdoor cooking.

But here's the sizzling question: Are YOU ready to become the grill master of your neighborhood? Imagine whipping up restaurant-worthy dishes on your Blackstone Griddle that leave your friends and family begging for seconds. This guide holds that power, with easy-to-follow recipes and expert techniques anyone can master.

Don't let your Blackstone knowledge gather dust! Turn those "oohs" and "aahs" at your next cookout into a wave of new Blackstone believers on Amazon. Here's your chance to be a hero: Head over to Amazon and leave a detailed review. Did this guide transform your backyard grilling? Did a specific recipe become your new favorite? Let the world know!

Feeling like a Blackstone rockstar? Snap a sizzling pic of your latest griddle creation or film a short video showcasing your skills. Share it with your review and become a legend in the Blackstone community on Amazon.

Remember, your review is pure gold. It helps others unlock the full potential of their Blackstone Griddle and become backyard grilling superstars themselves. Let's build a sizzling Blackstone community on Amazon, one rave review and mouthwatering recipe at a time!

Unlock Your Blackstone Griddle Bonus Content!
Scan & Supercharge Your Griddle-licious

Embracing the Blackstone Griddle: A Culinary Revolution on a Flattop

The Blackstone Griddle isn't just another grill; it's a game-changer in outdoor cooking. Forget the limitations of traditional grills with their uneven heat distribution and restricted cooking space. The Blackstone Griddle offers a vast, smooth surface that unlocks a world of culinary possibilities, transforming your backyard into a sizzling stage for delicious meals and unforgettable gatherings.

Introducing the Blackstone Griddle

Imagine a spacious, flat-top griddle powered by powerful burners. This is the heart of the Blackstone experience. It's a single, expansive surface that allows you to cook a variety of foods simultaneously and evenly. Unlike grills with grates, where smaller items can fall through, the griddle provides a secure platform for everything from delicate fish fillets to hearty burgers.

Advantages Over Traditional Grills

- **Unmatched Versatility**: The Blackstone Griddle goes beyond burgers and brats. You can sear steaks, fry eggs, cook pancakes, stir-fry vegetables, and even bake pizzas – all on the same surface! This opens doors to a wider culinary repertoire, making it perfect for adventurous cooks and those seeking variety.
- **Even Heat Distribution**: Say goodbye to hot and cold spots! The Blackstone's powerful burners ensure consistent heat across the entire griddle surface. This means perfectly cooked food, every time. No more overcooked edges or undercooked centers.
- **Effortless Cooking**: The smooth, flat surface allows for easy flipping and maneuvering of food. Spatulas glide effortlessly, making it a joy to cook on. Additionally, cleaning is a breeze – no more scraping through grates!
- **Increased Cooking Capacity**: The vast surface area of the griddle allows you to cook large quantities of food at once. This is ideal for feeding a crowd, whether it's a family gathering, a neighborhood cookout, or a tailgate party.

The Blackstone Griddle Lifestyle

Owning a Blackstone Griddle isn't just about cooking food; it's about embracing an outdoor culinary lifestyle. It's about transforming your patio into an extension of your kitchen, a place where friends and family gather around the sizzling flattop, sharing laughter, conversation, and of course, delicious meals.

Here are some defining elements of the Blackstone Griddle lifestyle:

- **Effortless Entertaining**: Impress your guests with an array of dishes cooked to perfection on your griddle. From breakfast feasts to sizzling fajitas and gourmet pizzas, the possibilities are endless.
- **Outdoor Cooking Made Easy**: Forget the complexity of charcoal or gas grills with their intricate setups. The Blackstone Griddle is easy to use, requiring minimal prep and offering intuitive temperature control. This allows you to focus on what matters most – enjoying time with loved ones.
- **A Culinary Canvas for Creativity**: The versatility of the griddle unlocks a world of culinary exploration. Experiment with different recipes, discover new flavors, and personalize your creations to match your and your guests' preferences.

The Features and Benefits of Blackstone Griddle: Unlocking Culinary Potential

The Blackstone Griddle comes in a variety of models, each catering to different cooking needs and preferences. Let's delve into the key features and their advantages to help you choose the perfect griddle for your culinary adventures.

A Griddle for Every Appetite

Blackstone offers griddles in a range of sizes, from compact tabletops perfect for balconies or tailgating, to expansive freestanding models that can handle a feast for a crowd. Here's a breakdown of popular sizes:

- **17" - 22" Griddles**: Ideal for small patios or balconies, these compact griddles offer enough space for whipping up breakfast for a few or sizzling up some burgers. Their portability makes them great for camping trips or picnics.
- **28" - 36" Griddles**: These mid-sized griddles are perfect for most backyards and patios. They provide ample space for cooking a variety of dishes simultaneously, making them ideal for family meals or gatherings with friends.
- **48" and Above**: These giants of the griddle world are perfect for catering events or feeding a large group. Imagine flipping pancakes for a hungry crowd or creating a fajita station where everyone can customize their own meals.

Powering Your Culinary Creations

The number and configuration of burners significantly impact your cooking experience. Here's what to consider:

- **Single Burner**: Ideal for smaller griddles, a single burner offers sufficient heat for basic cooking tasks.
- **Double Burner**: Most Blackstone griddles feature two H-shaped burners. This configuration allows for independent heat zones, perfect for creating a sear zone for steaks while keeping vegetables warm on a cooler area.
- **Four Burner**: Larger griddles may boast four burners, providing even more heat control and the ability to cook a wider variety of dishes simultaneously.

Hood Options for Added Convenience

Some Blackstone Griddles come equipped with a detachable hood. This offers several benefits:

- **Temperature Control**: The hood helps trap heat, allowing for more precise temperature control and quicker cooking times. It's ideal for recipes that require slow simmering or braising.
- **Wind Protection**: Cooking outdoors can be unpredictable. A hood protects your food from wind gusts that can affect heat distribution.
- **Smoke and Grease Management**: The hood helps contain smoke and grease splatter, keeping your cooking area cleaner and reducing smoke inhalation.

Key Components: Built for Performance

Beyond size and burners, several key components contribute to the Blackstone Griddle's functionality:

- **Griddle Top**: Made from heavy-duty rolled steel, the griddle top provides a large, smooth cooking surface that retains heat evenly. This allows for consistent cooking and easy flipping of food. The pre-seasoned surface ensures easy food release and simplifies cleaning.
- **Grease Management System**: Blackstone griddles feature a convenient grease management system. A channel at the edge of the griddle collects grease, which then flows into a removable grease tray. This keeps your cooking surface clean and prevents flare-ups.
- **Control Knobs**: Intuitive control knobs allow you to easily adjust the heat for different cooking needs. Some models even feature electronic ignition for a quick and convenient startup.

Matching Features to Your Cooking Style

The features you prioritize will depend on your cooking style. Here's a quick guide:

- **Frequent Entertainer**: Opt for a larger griddle with multiple burners and a hood for better temperature control and smoke management.
- **Camping Enthusiast**: Choose a compact, portable griddle for quick and easy meals on your outdoor adventures.
- **Balcony Griller**: A small tabletop griddle allows you to enjoy the Blackstone experience even in limited spaces.
- **Culinary Adventurer**: Consider a larger griddle with multiple burners to unlock the full potential of the griddle's versatility for various cooking styles.

By understanding the features and benefits of each Blackstone Griddle model, you can choose the perfect one to ignite your culinary creativity and turn your backyard into a sizzling hub for delicious memories.

Mastering the Controls of Your Blackstone Griddle

The control panel of your Blackstone Griddle holds the key to unlocking its full potential. Understanding the knobs, ignition system, and heat settings allows you to cook with precision and confidence. This chapter will guide you through these elements and provide safety precautions for a worry-free grilling experience.

Demystifying the Control Panel

- **Control Knobs**: Each burner on your griddle will have a corresponding control knob. These knobs typically rotate from "Off" to "High," with varying levels in between. The exact markings may differ slightly depending on your model.
- **Ignition System**: Most Blackstone Griddles feature an electronic ignition system for convenient startup. Simply press the designated igniter button while turning the desired control knob to "High." You may hear a clicking sound as the spark ignites the burner.
- **Heat Settings**: The control knobs correspond to different heat levels. These settings are not always labeled with specific temperatures but rather indicate the intensity of the flame.

A Heat Guide for Delicious Results

While specific temperatures may vary depending on your griddle model and outdoor conditions, here's a general heat setting guide for common foods:

- **Low (200°F - 300°F)**: Ideal for simmering sauces, keeping cooked foods warm, or melting cheese.
- **Medium (300°F - 400°F)**: Perfect for delicate foods like fish, pancakes, or grilled vegetables.
- **Medium-High (400°F - 500°F)**: Great for searing steaks, fajitas, or stir-frying.
- **High (500°F and Above)**: Use this setting for achieving a crispy crust on burgers or quickly boiling water.

Tips for Optimal Temperature Control

- **Preheating**: Always preheat your griddle for at least 10-15 minutes on medium heat before cooking. This ensures even heat distribution across the griddle top.
- **Two-Zone Cooking**: Many Blackstone Griddles have multiple burners, allowing you to create different heat zones. Use a higher heat setting on one side for searing and a lower heat on the other side for keeping food warm.
- **Adjusting the Flame**: Pay attention to the flame size while cooking. You can fine-tune the heat by slightly adjusting the control knob.

Safety First: Essential Precautions for Griddle Masters

Griddle safety is paramount. Here are some key precautions to remember:

- **Leak Check**: Before each use, perform a leak check. Turn on the gas supply and apply a soapy water solution to all gas line connections. Look for bubbles, which indicate a leak. If you find one, turn off the gas immediately and do not use the griddle. Contact a qualified technician for repair.
- **Keep it Clear**: Maintain a clear space of at least 3 feet around the griddle while cooking. This ensures proper ventilation and prevents flammable objects from coming into contact with the heat.
- **Never Leave Unattended**: Never leave your griddle unattended while it's lit. Keep a watchful eye on the flames and food to avoid flare-ups or grease fires.
- **Turn it Off**: When finished cooking, turn off all control knobs and ensure the flame is completely extinguished before turning off the gas supply.

By understanding the controls, following these safety precautions, and using the heat settings as a guide, you'll be well on your way to becoming a Blackstone Griddle master, creating delicious meals while keeping safety at the forefront of your grilling experience.

Mastering Your Griddle Experience: Tips, Tricks, and Techniques for Griddle Nirvana

Now that you've assembled your Blackstone Griddle, unlocked the controls, and understand safety protocols, it's time to delve into the world of griddle mastery! This chapter will equip you with essential tips and techniques to elevate your culinary creations and keep your griddle performing at its peak.

The Art of Seasoning

Seasoning your Blackstone Griddle is a crucial step for creating a non-stick surface and maximizing its performance. Here's how to properly season your griddle:

1. **Clean and Preheat**: Begin with a clean griddle top. Wash it with warm soapy water, rinse thoroughly, and dry completely. Preheat the griddle on medium heat for 10-15 minutes.
2. **Oil Application**: Using a high smoke point oil (vegetable oil, canola oil) and a paper towel, coat the entire griddle surface with a thin layer of oil.
3. **Heat and Wipe**: Turn the heat to high and let the oil shimmer for about 5 minutes. Wipe off any excess oil with a paper towel.
4. **Repeat**: Repeat steps 2 and 3 two to three more times, allowing the griddle to cool slightly between applications. This creates a layered, seasoned surface.
5. **Cooling Down**: Turn off the griddle and let it cool completely before storing or using.

Heat Zonation for Culinary Versatility

Blackstone Griddles with multiple burners offer the advantage of heat zonation. This allows you to cook various dishes simultaneously at their optimal temperatures:

- **Searing Zone**: Set one burner to high heat for searing steaks, burgers, or scallops.
- **Cooking Zone**: Maintain a medium or medium-low heat zone on another burner for cooking vegetables, eggs, or keeping cooked food warm.
- **Indirect Heat Zone**: Turn off a burner completely to create an indirect heat zone for slow-cooking delicate foods or melting cheese.

Griddle Flipping Finesse

Mastering the art of spatula work on your griddle takes practice, but with a few techniques, you'll be flipping like a pro:

- **The Right Tool**: Invest in a good quality griddle spatula. Look for one with a wide, sturdy blade and a long handle for leverage. A bevelled edge helps slide under food effortlessly.
- **The Gentle Approach**: Don't force the flip! Wait until food releases easily from the griddle surface before attempting to flip.
- **The Slide and Scoop**: Slide your spatula under the food, angling it slightly towards the flattop. With a gentle lift and a scooping motion, flip the food onto the other side.
- **Practice Makes Perfect**: Start with smaller, easier-to-flip items like pancakes or vegetables. As you gain confidence, you can tackle larger cuts of meat

Cleaning and Maintenance Hacks for a Long-Lasting Griddle

Proper cleaning and maintenance will keep your Blackstone Griddle in top condition for years to come. Here are some helpful hacks:

- **Post-Cook Cleaning**: While the griddle is still warm, but not too hot to touch, pour a cup of water on the surface. The hot water will loosen food particles, making them easier to scrape off with your spatula.
- **Scrub and Rinse**: Once the food particles are loose, use a grill brush to scrub the surface. Rinse thoroughly with clean water and dry completely with a paper towel.
- **Deep Cleaning**: For a deeper clean, you can use a baking soda paste (baking soda mixed with a little water) to scrub stubborn stains. Rinse thoroughly and dry completely.
- **Seasoning Touch-Up**: After deep cleaning or prolonged use, you may want to re-season your griddle with a light coat of oil to maintain its non-stick properties.
- **Lid Maintenance:** If your griddle has a hood, clean it regularly with soapy water. Apply a light coat of cooking oil on the hinges to prevent rust.
- **Storage Tips**: Store your griddle in a cool, dry place when not in use. Cover it with a grill cover to protect it from dust and moisture.

Equipping Your Griddle Arsenal: Tools and Accessories for Blackstone Mastery

Your Blackstone Griddle is a powerful culinary tool, but to unleash its full potential, you'll need the right arsenal. This chapter equips you with the essential tools and explores some recommended accessories to elevate your griddle experience.

Essential Tools for Griddle Domination

While your Blackstone Griddle comes ready to cook, a few key tools will make your experience smoother and more enjoyable:

- **Turners and Spatulas**: These are your griddle warriors. Invest in a sturdy turner with a wide, flat surface for flipping burgers, pancakes, and other flat foods. A long-handled spatula with a bevelled edge allows for easy maneuvering and scooping under food. Consider having a dedicated fish spatula for delicate items.
- **Griddle Scraper**: As food cooks, bits and pieces will stick to the griddle surface. A griddle scraper, with a long handle and a wide, flat blade, helps remove these remnants efficiently while the griddle is still warm.
- **Spray Bottle**: A spray bottle filled with water is a handy tool for deglazing the griddle after cooking. The hot water loosens stuck-on food particles, making cleaning a breeze. You can also use it to control flare-ups by spritzing a small amount of water on flames.

Recommended Accessories for Enhanced Functionality

Several accessories can further enhance your Blackstone Griddle experience and unlock new culinary possibilities:

- **Griddle Cover**: A griddle cover protects your griddle from dust, rain, and UV rays when not in use. It also helps retain heat during cooking, especially when using the hood.
- **Griddle Press**: This heavy cast-iron tool applies even pressure to your food, resulting in perfectly seared burgers, crispy grilled sandwiches, and evenly cooked paninis.
- **Wok Ring**: Transform your griddle into a mini stir-fry station! A wok ring creates a well for stir-fries, keeping ingredients contained and allowing for efficient heat distribution.
- **Griddle Topper**: This versatile accessory provides an extra elevated cooking surface, perfect for creating small pizzas, cookies, or delicate appetizers that require indirect heat.
- **Cutting Board and Knife Set**: Having a dedicated cutting board and knife set near your griddle allows for convenient prep work and ingredient chopping while you cook.
- **Utensil Holder**: Keep your spatulas and turners organized and within easy reach with a magnetic utensil holder attached to the side of your griddle.
- **Griddle Grilling Baskets**: These perforated baskets allow you to easily grill small items like vegetables, shrimp, or kabobs without worrying about them falling through the grates (if your griddle has them).
- **Grease Management Accessories**: Depending on your griddle model, additional grease management accessories like grease can liners or a grease management hose extension can simplify the cleaning process.

Choosing the Right Tools and Accessories

When selecting tools and accessories, consider your cooking style and the types of dishes you plan to create on your griddle. Don't overwhelm yourself – start with the essentials and add on as you explore different culinary adventures with your Blackstone Griddle. Remember, quality tools will make your cooking experience more enjoyable and efficient.

By equipping yourself with the right tools and exploring the world of griddle accessories, you'll be well on your way to becoming a Blackstone Griddle master, ready to tackle any recipe and create restaurant-quality meals at home.

Maintaining Your Griddle Mastery: Care, Troubleshooting, and the Road Ahead

Your Blackstone Griddle is a culinary powerhouse, but like any good tool, it requires proper care and maintenance to perform at its peak. This chapter will guide you through essential cleaning and storage techniques, equip you to troubleshoot common griddle issues, and inspire you to continue your griddle mastery journey.

Ensuring Long-Lasting Performance: Cleaning and Storage Essentials

Taking the time to clean and store your Blackstone Griddle properly will extend its lifespan and keep it looking its best.

Here are some key practices:

- **Post-Cook Cleaning**: While the griddle is still warm (but not too hot to touch), pour a cup of water on the surface. The hot water loosens food particles, making them easier to scrape off with a griddle scraper.

- **Scrub and Rinse**: Once the food particles are loose, use a grill brush to scrub the surface. Rinse thoroughly with clean water and dry completely with a paper towel. Avoid using harsh soaps or scouring pads, as they can damage the seasoned surface.
- **Deep Cleaning**: For a deeper clean, you can use a baking soda paste (baking soda mixed with a little water) to scrub stubborn stains. Rinse thoroughly and dry completely.
- **Seasoning Touch-Up**: After deep cleaning or prolonged use, you may want to re-season your griddle with a light coat of oil to maintain its non-stick properties.
- **Lid Maintenance (if applicable)**: Clean the hood regularly with soapy water. Apply a light coat of cooking oil on the hinges to prevent rust.
- **Storage Tips**: Store your griddle in a cool, dry place when not in use. Cover it with a griddle cover to protect it from dust and moisture.

The Road Ahead: A World of Griddle Exploration

Your Blackstone Griddle is a gateway to endless culinary possibilities. Here are some ways to keep exploring and expanding your griddle mastery:

- **Griddle Community**: Join online communities and forums dedicated to Blackstone Griddle enthusiasts. Share recipes, tips, and troubleshoot challenges with fellow griddle masters.
- **Experimentation is Key**: Don't be afraid to experiment! The versatility of the griddle allows you to try new recipes and techniques.
- **Master Different Cuisines**: From sizzling fajitas to fluffy Japanese pancakes (okonomiyaki), your griddle can handle a wide range of cuisines.
- **Become a Griddle Entertaining Pro**: Impress your guests with delicious griddle creations at your next gathering. The Blackstone Griddle is perfect for creating interactive cooking experiences and fostering memorable moments around the flattop.

Troubleshooting and FAQs: Conquering Griddle Challenges with Confidence

Your Blackstone Griddle is a powerful and versatile cooking tool, but even the most seasoned griddle chefs might encounter a few bumps along the road. This chapter addresses frequently asked questions (FAQs) and troubleshooting tips to keep you grilling with confidence.

FAQs: Demystifying Griddle Use

1. **What oil should I use to season my griddle?** Use a high smoke point oil like vegetable oil, canola oil, or avocado oil for seasoning.
2. **How often should I re-season my griddle?** Re-seasoning is necessary after deep cleaning or prolonged use. You can also re-season after a long period of non-use. A light coat of oil applied after cleaning and wiped clean will suffice.
3. **Can I use soap on my griddle?** Avoid using harsh soaps or detergents on your griddle top, as they can damage the seasoned surface. Opt for hot water and a grill brush for regular cleaning. For stubborn stains, use a baking soda paste.
4. **What is the best way to clean the grease trap?** Empty the grease trap after each use. You can also line it with aluminum foil for easier cleanup. Some models have removable grease cups that can be washed with soap and water.
5. **Can I use my griddle indoors?** Blackstone griddles are primarily designed for outdoor use due to the heat they generate. If using indoors, ensure proper ventilation and follow all safety precautions in your user manual. Some models may have specific warnings against indoor use, so be sure to check.

Troubleshooting Common Griddle Issues

Uneven Heat Distribution:
Solution: Check burner placement for proper alignment. Ensure the griddle top is clean and free of debris. If outdoors, use a wind barrier to minimize temperature fluctuations.

Stuck-on Food:
Solution: Re-season your griddle if food sticks excessively. Also, preheat the griddle to the appropriate temperature before cooking. Using a spatula with a wide, flat surface helps maneuver food easily.

Flare-Ups:
Solution: Trim excess fat from meats before cooking. Keep the griddle surface clean of grease buildup. A spray bottle filled with water can be used to control minor flare-ups. Never pour water directly on the flames.

Ignition Issues:
Solution: Check for a faulty connection or a dead battery (in some models). Consult the user manual for troubleshooting steps or contact Blackstone customer service.

Gas Leak Suspicion:
Solution: Do not attempt to use the griddle. Turn off the gas supply immediately and contact a qualified technician for repair. Never ignore a suspected gas leak.

Additional Tips

- **Consult the User Manual**: Your Blackstone Griddle user manual is a valuable resource. It contains assembly instructions, specific cleaning and maintenance recommendations for your model, and troubleshooting tips tailored to your griddle's features.
- **Blackstone Customer Service**: If you encounter an issue you can't resolve yourself, don't hesitate to contact Blackstone customer service. They can provide expert advice and troubleshooting assistance.

By understanding these FAQs and troubleshooting tips, you'll be well-equipped to handle most griddle challenges that may arise. Remember, the Blackstone Griddle community is here to support you. Explore online forums and resources to learn from other griddle enthusiasts and share your own experiences. So, fire up your griddle with confidence, and get ready to conquer any culinary challenge that comes your way!

GRIDDLE UP YOUR MORNINGS
BREAKFAST DELIGHTS

The aroma of sizzling bacon and fluffy pancakes wafting through the air – there's nothing quite like a delicious breakfast to kick off your day. But who says breakfast needs to be confined to the kitchen? Your Blackstone griddle can become your outdoor breakfast haven, offering a fun and flavorful way to fuel your mornings.

This chapter takes you on a journey through a variety of breakfast options, from classic favorites like pancakes and scrambled eggs to creative twists like breakfast burritos and quesadillas. Whether you're craving something sweet, savory, or protein-packed, these recipes will transform your Blackstone griddle into a breakfast powerhouse.

So, fire up your griddle, grab your favorite ingredients, and get ready to experience breakfast in a whole new way!

Alex & Jamie
Blake

SIZZLING BACON, EGG & CHEESE BREAKFAST BURRITOS

SERVES 4

PREP TIME 10 mins

COOK TIME 15 mins

Alex & Jamie
Blake

Here's what you'll need

- 8 slices bacon, cooked and crumbled
- 8 large eggs, scrambled
- 1 cup shredded cheddar cheese
- 4 large flour tortillas
- Salsa, sour cream, and avocado (optional toppings)

Ready to get cooking? Let's go!

1. Preheat your griddle to medium heat.
2. Scramble the eggs in a bowl with a splash of milk and salt & pepper to taste.
3. Warm the tortillas on the griddle for about 30 seconds per side.
4. Spread scrambled eggs evenly on each tortilla, followed by crumbled bacon and a sprinkle of cheese.
5. Fold the bottom of the tortilla up, then fold in the sides, creating a burrito shape.
6. Cook for 1-2 minutes per side, or until golden brown and cheese is melted.
7. Serve immediately with your favorite toppings.

Tips

- Feeling spicy? Add chopped jalapeños to your scrambled eggs.
- For a veggie twist, throw in some sauteed peppers and onions with the bacon.
- Get creative with your cheese! Try pepper jack, Monterey Jack, or even crumbled queso fresco.

Nutritional Information (per serving)

Calories: 450, **Fat**: 25g, **Protein**: 20g, **Carbs**: 30g

Craving a hearty and satisfying breakfast? Look no further than these sizzling bacon, egg, and cheese burritos! Made on your trusty Blackstone Griddle, this recipe is quick, easy, and endlessly customizable. Packed with protein and flavor, it's the perfect way to fuel your mornings.

GRIDDLE-FRIED HASH BROWNS WITH PEPPERS AND ONIONS

Here's what you'll need

- 4 large russet potatoes, peeled and shredded
- 1 bell pepper, chopped
- 1/2 onion, chopped
- 1 tbsp olive oil
- Salt & pepper to taste

SERVES
4

PREP TIME
5 mins

COOK TIME
15 mins

Let's get griddle-ing!

1. Preheat your griddle to medium heat.
2. In a large bowl, toss shredded potatoes with olive oil, salt, and pepper.
3. Spread the potato mixture evenly on the preheated griddle, forming a large patty.
4. Add chopped peppers and onions on top of the potato mixture.
5. Press down gently with a spatula to help everything stick together.
6. Cook for 5-7 minutes per side, or until golden brown and crispy.
7. Use a spatula to cut the hash browns into squares for easier serving.

Tips

- For extra crispy hash browns, preheat your griddle to medium-high heat and use a griddle press (if you have one) during cooking.
- Feeling adventurous? Add chopped ham, sausage, or even shredded cheese to your hash brown mixture.
- Want to go vegetarian? Swap the bacon for chopped mushrooms

Alex & Jamie
Blake

Nutritional Information
(per serving)

Calories: 250, **Fat**: 10g,
Protein: 5g, **Carbs**: 35g

Craving crispy, golden hash browns but tired of the stovetop splatter? Your Blackstone Griddle is here to save the day! This recipe is simple, flavorful, and perfect for a crowd.

SWEET AND SAVORY SAUSAGE AND PANCAKE SKEWERS

SERVES
4

PREP TIME
10 mins

COOK TIME
15 mins

Alex & Jamie
Blake

Here's what you'll need

- 1 package breakfast sausage links, cut into bite-sized pieces
- 1 cup pancake mix (your favorite brand)
- Milk (according to pancake mix instructions)
- 1 cup mixed berries
- Wooden skewers

Let's skewer some breakfast magic!

1. Preheat your griddle to medium heat.
2. Prepare pancake batter according to package instructions.
3. Thread sausage pieces, berries, and small scoops of pancake batter onto wooden skewers, alternating ingredients.
4. Lightly oil the griddle and cook skewers for 3-4 minutes per side, or until sausage is cooked through and pancakes are golden brown

Tips

- Get creative with your skewers! Try adding chopped apple, pineapple, or even chocolate chips to the mix.
- For a fun twist, use pre-made pancake batter to save time.
- Make sure your sausage is cooked through before serving. You can pre-cook the sausage on the griddle for added convenience.

Nutritional Information
(per serving)

Calories: 400, **Fat**: 20g,
Protein: 15g, **Carbs**: 40g

Breakfast on a stick? Yes, please! These fun and flavorful skewers combine sweet and savory flavors for a unique and delicious morning treat. Perfect for kids and adults alike, this recipe is easy to customize and sure to be a crowd-pleaser.

SPICY CHORIZO BREAKFAST SCRAMBLE WITH AVOCADO

SERVES 2

PREP TIME 5 mins

COOK TIME 10 mins

Alex & Jamie Blake

Here's what you'll need

- 4 oz Mexican chorizo sausage, casings removed and crumbled
- 2 large eggs, scrambled
- 1/2 cup chopped bell pepper (any color)
- 1/4 cup chopped onion
- 1/4 cup crumbled feta cheese
- 1/2 ripe avocado, sliced
- 1 tbsp olive oil
- Salt & pepper to taste

Let's get cooking!

1. Preheat your griddle to medium heat.
2. Heat olive oil on the griddle. Add crumbled chorizo sausage and cook until browned and crispy, breaking it up with a spatula as it cooks (about 3-4 minutes).
3. Add chopped bell pepper and onion to the griddle with the cooked chorizo. Sauté for another 2-3 minutes, or until softened and slightly browned.
4. Pour the scrambled eggs over the chorizo, vegetables, and cheese mixture on the griddle.
5. Season with salt and pepper to taste.
6. Using a spatula, gently fold the scrambled egg mixture with the other ingredients until almost set.
7. Remove from heat and serve immediately on plates. Top with sliced avocado.

Tips

- Craving more heat? Add a pinch of cayenne pepper or a chopped jalapeño to the chorizo.
- For a creamier scramble, whisk in a splash of milk or cream cheese to your eggs.
- Make it a complete meal! Serve with toast, tortillas, or breakfast potatoes.

Nutritional Information
(per serving)

Calories: 820, **Fat**: 55g,
Protein: 35g, **Carbs**: 27g

Kickstart your day with this vibrant scramble! Mexican chorizo brings the heat, while creamy avocado adds a cool contrast. It's all cooked to perfection on your trusty Blackstone Griddle for a protein-packed and flavorful breakfast.

BACON, EGG, AND CHEESE BREAKFAST QUESADILLAS

SERVES 2

PREP TIME 5 mins

COOK TIME 10 mins

Alex & Jamie
Blake

Here's what you'll need

- 4 large flour tortillas
- 4 slices bacon, cooked and crumbled
- 2 large eggs, scrambled
- 1/2 cup shredded cheddar cheese
- Salsa and sour cream (optional toppings)

Let's get griddle-ing!

1. Preheat your griddle to medium heat.
2. Spread a thin layer of cheese on half of each tortilla.
3. Top with scrambled eggs and crumbled bacon.
4. Fold the tortilla in half, enclosing the filling.
5. Cook for 2-3 minutes per side, or until golden brown and cheese is melted.
6. Cut into wedges and serve with salsa and sour cream, if desired.

Tips

- Feeling adventurous? Add chopped veggies like bell peppers or onions to your scramble.
- Get cheesy! Experiment with different types of shredded cheese, like pepper jack or Monterey Jack.
- Leftover sausage or shredded chicken can also be used as a protein filling.

Nutritional Information
(per serving)

Calories: 500, **Fat**: 30g,
Protein: 25g, **Carbs**: 35g

Craving a breakfast that's both satisfying and simple? These bacon, egg, and cheese quesadillas are your answer! They're quick to whip up on your Blackstone Griddle, perfect for busy mornings. Plus, they're endlessly customizable to fit your taste.

FLUFFY BUTTERMILK PANCAKES WITH MAPLE SYRUP AND BERRIES

Here's what you'll need

- 1 cup all-purpose flour
- 2 tbsp sugar
- 2 tsp baking powder
- 1/4 tsp salt
- 1 1/4 cups buttermilk
- 1 egg
- 1 tbsp melted butter
- Maple syrup and fresh berries (for serving)

SERVES
2 - 3

PREP TIME
5 mins

COOK TIME
10 mins

Alex & Jamie
Blake

Let's get griddle-ing!

1. Preheat your griddle to medium-low heat.
2. In a large bowl, whisk together flour, sugar, baking powder, and salt.
3. In a separate bowl, whisk together buttermilk, egg, and melted butter.
4. Pour the wet ingredients into the dry ingredients and whisk just until combined (a few lumps are okay).
5. Lightly grease the griddle. Pour batter onto the griddle in desired sizes, leaving space between pancakes for spreading.
6. Cook for 2-3 minutes per side, or until bubbles appear on the surface and the edges start to set.
7. Flip the pancakes and cook for another 1-2 minutes, or until golden brown.
8. Serve immediately with maple syrup and fresh berries.

Tips

- For thicker pancakes, use slightly less buttermilk.
- Want fluffy pancakes? Don't overmix your batter!
- Don't press down on the pancakes while they cook.
- Spruce them up! Add chocolate chips, chopped nuts, or even fruit slices to your batter.

Nutritional Information
(per serving)

Calories: 350, **Fat**: 15g,
Protein: 8g, **Carbs**: 45g

Light, fluffy, and bursting with buttermilk flavor, these pancakes are a breakfast dream come true! Made on your Blackstone Griddle, they're a breeze to whip up and even easier to devour.

SPICY CHORIZO BREAKFAST TACOS WITH AVOCADO CREMA

SERVES
2

PREP TIME
10 mins

COOK TIME
15 mins

Alex & Jamie
Blake

Nutritional Information
(per serving)
Calories: 500, **Fat**: 30g,
Protein: 20g, **Carbs**: 30g

Spice up your breakfast routine with these protein-packed chorizo tacos! Made on your griddle with creamy avocado crema and fresh toppings, they're a delicious and satisfying way to fuel your mornings.

Here's what you'll need

For the Avocado Crema:
- 1/2 ripe avocado, mashed
- 1/4 cup sour cream
- 1 tbsp lime juice
- 1/4 tsp chopped fresh cilantro
- Salt & pepper to taste

For the Tacos:
- 2 small flour tortillas
- 2 oz Mexican chorizo sausage, casings removed and crumbled
- 1/2 cup scrambled eggs
- 1/4 cup shredded pepper jack cheese
- Chopped cherry tomatoes, chopped red onion, and fresh cilantro (for serving)

Let's get cooking!

1. Preheat your griddle to medium heat.
2. For the Avocado Crema: In a small bowl, mash together avocado, sour cream, lime juice, and chopped cilantro. Season with salt and pepper to taste. Set aside.
3. For the Tacos: Cook chorizo sausage on the griddle until browned and cooked through.
4. Add scrambled eggs to the griddle and cook until almost set.
5. Warm the tortillas on the griddle for about 30 seconds per side.
6. Spoon scrambled eggs and chorizo sausage onto each tortilla.
7. Sprinkle with shredded pepper jack cheese.
8. Fold the tortillas in half (or fold one side over the filling to create an open-faced taco).
9. Cook for another 1-2 minutes, or until cheese is melted and tortillas are slightly golden brown.
10. Serve immediately with avocado crema, chopped cherry tomatoes, chopped red onion, and fresh cilantro.

Tips

- Don't like it spicy? Skip the chorizo or use a milder sausage.
- Add other veggies like bell peppers or sauteed onions to your taco filling.
- Swap the pepper jack cheese for another type like cheddar or Monterey Jack.
- Leftover taco filling can be used for breakfast burritos the next day!

13

BLACKSTONE BITES & SIDES
GRIDDLE-SIZED GOODNESS TO SET THE STAGE

Fire up your Blackstone griddle and get ready to transform your next gathering! This chapter dives into a world of sizzling appetizers and delectable sides, all perfectly suited for the unique capabilities of your griddle, we'll unlock the full potential of your griddle as an appetizer and side dish powerhouse.

These recipes are designed to be easy to prepare and perfect for sharing. Whether you're hosting a backyard barbecue, a casual get-together, or a festive holiday celebration, this chapter equips you with the culinary tools to impress your guests with every bite. So, grab your ingredients, preheat your griddle, and get ready to elevate your appetizer and side dish game to a whole new level!

Alex & Jamie
Blake

CHEESY GARLIC BREAD WITH CRISPY BACON

SERVES
4 - 6

PREP TIME
5 mins

COOK TIME
5 mins

Alex & Jamie
Blake

Here's what you'll need

- 1 French baguette, sliced into 1-inch thick slices
- 1/4 cup unsalted butter, softened
- 2 cloves garlic, minced
- 1/4 cup grated Parmesan cheese
- 1/4 cup shredded mozzarella cheese
- 4 slices bacon, cooked crisp and crumbled
- Fresh parsley (for garnish, optional)

Let's get griddle-ing!

1. Preheat your griddle to medium heat.
2. In a small bowl, combine softened butter, minced garlic, Parmesan cheese, and mozzarella cheese.
3. Spread the cheese mixture generously on one side of each bread slice.
4. Place the bread slices, cheese side down, on the preheated griddle.
5. Cook for 2-3 minutes, or until the cheese melts and the bottom of the bread starts to brown.
6. Flip the bread slices and top with crumbled cooked bacon.
7. Cook for another 1-2 minutes, or until the other side is golden brown and crispy.
8. Garnish with fresh parsley (optional) and serve immediately.

Nutritional Information (per serving)

Calories: 300, **Fat**: 20g,
Protein: 10g, **Carbs**: 30g

A classic side dish elevated by the griddle's ability to achieve perfect crispness.

SPICY KOREAN GLAZED BRUSSELS SPROUTS

SERVES 4

PREP TIME 10 mins

COOK TIME 10 mins

Alex & Jamie Blake

Here's what you'll need

- 1 pound Brussels sprouts, trimmed and halved
- 1 tbsp olive oil
- 2 tbsp soy sauce
- 1 tbsp brown sugar
- 1 tbsp Sriracha (adjust to your spice preference)
- 1 tbsp rice vinegar
- 1 clove garlic, minced
- 1 tsp grated ginger
- 1 tbsp white sesame seeds, toasted

Let's get griddle-ing!

1. Preheat your griddle to medium-high heat. Add the olive oil.
2. Sauté the halved Brussels sprouts for 5-7 minutes, or until slightly softened and starting to brown.
3. In a small bowl, whisk together soy sauce, brown sugar, Sriracha, rice vinegar, minced garlic, and grated ginger to create the glaze.
4. Pour the glaze over the Brussels sprouts on the griddle and toss to coat evenly.
5. Cook for another 2-3 minutes, or until the glaze thickens and becomes sticky.
6. Remove from the heat and sprinkle with toasted sesame seeds.
7. Serve hot and enjoy the sweet, savory, and spicy flavor combination.

Nutritional Information
(per serving)

Calories: 200, **Fat**: 10g,
Protein: 5g, **Carbs**: 20g

An addictive side dish with a delightful mix of sweet, savory, and spicy.

GARLIC PARMESAN ASPARAGUS FRIES

SERVES 4

PREP TIME 5 mins

COOK TIME 5 mins

Alex & Jamie Blake

Here's what you'll need

- 1 pound asparagus spears, trimmed
- 1 tbsp olive oil
- 1/4 cup grated Parmesan cheese
- 1/4 tsp garlic powder
- Salt & pepper to taste

Let's get griddle-ing!

1. Preheat your griddle to medium-high heat. Add the olive oil.
2. Toss the asparagus spears with olive oil to coat them lightly.
3. Arrange the asparagus spears in a single layer on the preheated griddle.
4. Cook for 3-4 minutes per side, or until tender-crisp (adjust cooking time depending on the thickness of the asparagus).
5. Sprinkle with grated Parmesan cheese, garlic powder, salt, and pepper while the asparagus is still hot.
6. Serve immediately and enjoy the crispy texture and cheesy flavor.

Nutritional Information (per serving)

Calories: 150, **Fat**: 10g, **Protein**: 5g, **Carbs**: 10g

A healthy and flavorful alternative to french fries, perfect for dipping.

SMOKY CHIPOTLE SHRIMP SKEWERS WITH GRILLED PINEAPPLE

SERVES
2 - 3

PREP TIME
15 mins

COOK TIME
10 mins

Here's what you'll need

- 1 pound large shrimp, peeled and deveined
- 1 tbsp olive oil
- 1 tbsp lime juice
- 1 tsp chipotle chili powder
- 1/2 tsp smoked paprika
- 1/4 tsp ground cumin
- Salt & pepper to taste
- 1 pineapple, cut into chunks
- Wooden skewers (soaked in water for at least 30 minutes to prevent burning)

Let's get griddle-ing!

1. Preheat your griddle to medium-high heat. If it has a low setting, preheat to around 225°F for a smoky effect. If not, use a smoker box filled with wood chips.
2. In a bowl, whisk together olive oil, lime juice, chipotle chili powder, smoked paprika, ground cumin, salt, and pepper to create a marinade.
3. Add the shrimp to the marinade and toss to coat evenly. Marinate for at least 15 minutes.
4. Thread the marinated shrimp onto soaked wooden skewers.
5. If using a smoker box, add wood chips according to the manufacturer's instructions.
6. Place the skewers and pineapple chunks on the preheated griddle.
7. Cook the shrimp skewers for 3-4 minutes per side, or until opaque and cooked through.
8. Cook the pineapple chunks for 2-3 minutes per side, or until slightly caramelized.
9. Serve the smoky chipotle shrimp skewers hot with the grilled pineapple chunks.

Alex & Jamie
Blake

Nutritional Information
(per serving)

Calories: 400, **Fat**: 20g,
Protein: 35g, **Carbs**: 20g

A light and flavorful appetizer with a touch of smokiness.

SEARED SCALLOPS WITH LEMON BUTTER SAUCE

- 1 pound sea scallops
- 1 tbsp olive oil
- Salt & pepper to taste

For the Lemon Butter Sauce:

- 2 tbsp unsalted butter
- 1 tbsp lemon juice
- 1 clove garlic, minced
- 1/4 cup chopped fresh parsley

SERVES
2 - 3

PREP TIME
10 mins

COOK TIME
5 mins

Alex & Jamie
Blake

Let's get griddle-ing!

1. Pat the sea scallops dry with paper towels. Season generously with salt and pepper.
2. Preheat your griddle to medium-high heat. Add the olive oil.
3. Sear the scallops for 2-3 minutes per side, or until golden brown and cooked through (depending on thickness, the internal temperature for sea scallops should be around 145°F).
4. While the scallops cook, prepare the lemon butter sauce by melting butter in a small pan over low heat. Add lemon juice, minced garlic, and chopped fresh parsley. Swirl to combine.
5. Remove the cooked scallops from the griddle and place them on a plate.
6. Spoon the lemon butter sauce over the cooked scallops and serve immediately.

Nutritional Information
(per serving)

Calories: 350, **Fat**: 25g,
Protein: 20g, **Carbs**: 5g

An elegant and impressive appetizer cooked to perfection on your Blackstone griddle.

CRISPY BACON-WRAPPED JALAPEÑO POPPERS

SERVES
4 - 6

PREP TIME
10 mins

COOK TIME
5 mins

Alex & Jamie
Blake

Here's what you'll need

- 12 jalapeño peppers, halved, seeded, and membranes removed (wear gloves for handling peppers)
- 1/2 cup cream cheese, softened
- 1/4 cup shredded cheddar cheese
- 4 slices bacon, cooked crisp and crumbled
- 1/4 cup chopped fresh chives
  Toothpicks

Let's get griddle-ing!

1. Preheat your griddle to medium heat.
2. In a small bowl, combine softened cream cheese, shredded cheddar cheese, and chopped fresh chives. Mix well to create a filling.
3. Stuff each jalapeño pepper half with a generous amount of the cream cheese mixture.
4. Wrap a piece of cooked and crumbled bacon around each stuffed jalapeño half, securing it with a toothpick if needed.
5. Place the bacon-wrapped jalapeño poppers on the preheated griddle.
6. Cook for 2-3 minutes per side, or until the bacon is crispy and the filling is heated through.
7. Serve hot and enjoy the contrasting textures of crispy bacon and creamy cheese with a kick of spice from the jalapeños.

Nutritional Information
(per serving)
Calories: 350, **Fat**: 25g,
Protein: 20g, **Carbs**: 5g

A spicy and addictive appetizer that's guaranteed to disappear quickly.

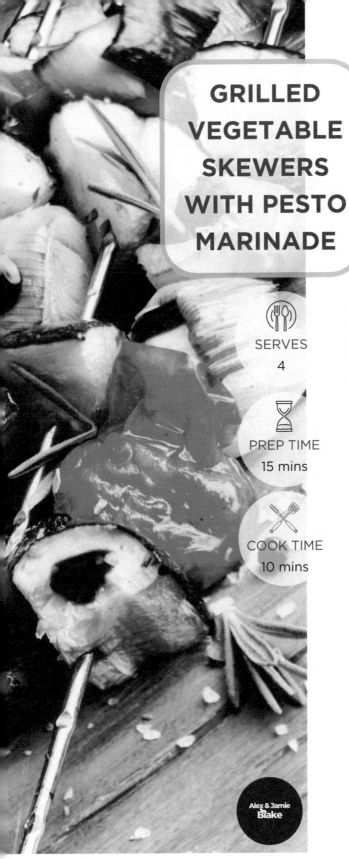

GRILLED VEGETABLE SKEWERS WITH PESTO MARINADE

SERVES
4

PREP TIME
15 mins

COOK TIME
10 mins

Alex & Jamie
Blake

Here's what you'll need

- 1 zucchini, cut into chunks
- 1 red bell pepper, cut into chunks
- 1 yellow bell pepper, cut into chunks
- 1 red onion, cut into wedges
- 1 cup cherry tomatoes
- 1/4 cup prepared pesto
- 1 tbsp olive oil
- Salt & pepper to taste
- Wooden skewers (soaked in water for at least 30 minutes to prevent burning)

Let's get griddle-ing!

1. In a bowl, whisk together pesto and olive oil to create a marinade.
2. Add the zucchini chunks, bell pepper chunks, red onion wedges, and cherry tomatoes to the marinade and toss to coat evenly.
3. Thread the marinated vegetables onto soaked wooden skewers.
4. Preheat your griddle to medium-high heat.
5. Place the vegetable skewers on the preheated griddle.
6. Cook for 5-7 minutes per side, or until the vegetables are tender-crisp and slightly charred.
7. Season with additional salt and pepper to taste (optional).
8. Serve the grilled vegetable skewers hot and enjoy the fresh flavors and vibrant colors.

Nutritional Information
(per serving)

Calories: 250, **Fat**: 15g,
Protein: 5g, **Carbs**: 20g

A colorful and flavorful vegetarian appetizer with a burst of fresh herbs.

GRIDDLE-ROASTED VEGGIE SYMPHONY
A CELEBRATION OF COLOR AND FLAVOR

Vegetables are the heart and soul of a healthy diet, but sometimes their preparation can feel monotonous. Enter the Blackstone griddle, your new stage for creating a vibrant symphony of roasted vegetables! This chapter unlocks a world of possibilities, showcasing how your griddle can transform simple vegetables into flavorful side dishes, vegetarian main courses, or even colorful toppings for other creations.

Alex & Jamie
Blake

GRILLED VEGETABLE SKEWERS WITH LEMON HERB MARINADE

SERVES
4

PREP TIME
15 mins

COOK TIME
10 mins

Alex & Jamie
Blake

Here's what you'll need

- 1 red bell pepper, cut into chunks
- 1 yellow bell pepper, cut into chunks
- 1 red onion, cut into wedges
- 1 zucchini, cut into thick slices
- 1 cup cherry tomatoes
- 1/4 cup olive oil
- 2 tbsp lemon juice
- 1 tbsp dried oregano
- 1 tsp garlic powder
- 1/2 tsp salt
- 1/4 tsp black pepper
- Wooden skewers

Let's get griddle-ing!

1. In a bowl, whisk together olive oil, lemon juice, oregano, garlic powder, salt, and pepper. Add vegetables and toss to coat.
2. Marinate vegetables for at least 15 minutes, or up to 30 minutes for deeper flavor.
3. Preheat your griddle to medium-high heat. Thread vegetables onto skewers, alternating colors and textures for visual appeal.
4. Grill skewers for 5-7 minutes per side, or until tender-crisp and slightly charred.
5. Serve immediately with your favorite dipping sauce, like balsamic glaze or hummus.

Tips

- Soak wooden skewers in water for 30 minutes before grilling to prevent burning.
- Pre-cut veggies into similar sizes for even cooking.
- Grill leftover marinated veggies on burgers or flatbreads!

Nutritional Information
(per serving)

Calories: 200, **Fat**: 10g,
Protein: 2g, **Carbs**: 20g

Kickstart your Blackstone grilling with these easy veggie skewers! Customizable with your favorites, they're a light and flavorful intro to griddle veggies.

SMOKY CHIPOTLE ROASTED CORN WITH COTIJA CHEESE

SERVES
4

PREP TIME
10 mins

COOK TIME
15 mins

Alex & Jamie
Blake

Here's what you'll need

- 4 ears fresh corn, husks removed and silks cleaned
- 1 tbsp olive oil
- 1 tsp chipotle chili powder
- 1/2 tsp smoked paprika
- 1/4 tsp garlic powder
- 1/4 tsp salt
- 1/4 cup crumbled cotija cheese
- Fresh cilantro (optional, for garnish)

Let's get griddle-ing!

1. Preheat your griddle to medium heat. In a bowl, toss corn cobs with olive oil, chipotle chili powder, smoked paprika, garlic powder, and salt.
2. Place corn cobs directly on the preheated griddle. Cook for 5-7 minutes per side, or until kernels are tender and lightly charred.
3. Remove corn from the griddle and sprinkle with crumbled cotija cheese. Garnish with fresh cilantro, if desired.

Tips

- Soak husks in water for 10 minutes before grilling for extra moist corn.
- Brush corn with melted butter for a richer flavor.
- Leftover corn kernels can be added to salads or salsas.

Nutritional Information
(per serving)

Calories: 250, **Fat**: 15g,
Protein: 5g, **Carbs**: 30g

Craving a side dish that's sweet, smoky, and cheesy? Look no further than this chipotle corn recipe! It's a crowd-pleaser perfect for your next griddle cookout.

GARLICKY GREEN BEANS WITH CRISPY SHALLOTS

Here's what you'll need

- 1 pound fresh green beans, trimmed
- 2 tbsp olive oil
- 2 cloves garlic, minced
- 1/2 shallot, thinly sliced
- 1/4 tsp salt
- 1/4 tsp black pepper

SERVES
4

PREP TIME
10 mins

COOK TIME
10 mins

Let's get griddle-ing!

1. Preheat your griddle to medium-high heat. Toss green beans with olive oil, garlic, salt, and pepper.
2. Spread green beans evenly on the preheated griddle. Cook for 5-7 minutes per side, or until tender-crisp and slightly blistered.
3. Add sliced shallots to the griddle and cook for an additional 2-3 minutes, or until golden brown and crispy.
4. Serve green beans with crispy shallots on top.

Tips

- Trim the ends of the green beans for even cooking.
- Use a mandoline slicer for perfectly thin and crispy shallots.
- Leftover shallots can be used as a topping for salads or other dishes.

Alex & Jamie
Blake

Nutritional Information (per serving)

Calories: 150, **Fat**: 10g,
Protein: 2g, **Carbs**: 15g

Simple doesn't have to be boring! These garlicky green beans with crispy shallots are a delightful side dish with a satisfying crunch. Perfect for your next griddle meal.

GRILLED PORTOBELLO MUSHROOM STEAKS WITH BALSAMIC GLAZE

SERVES 2

PREP TIME 10 mins

COOK TIME 15 mins

Alex & Jamie
Blake

Here's what you'll need

- 2 large portobello mushrooms, stems removed
- 1/4 cup balsamic vinegar
- 2 tbsp olive oil
- 1 tbsp fresh thyme leaves (or 1 tsp dried thyme)
- 1/2 tsp garlic powder
- 1/4 tsp salt
- 1/4 tsp black pepper
- 1/4 cup crumbled goat cheese (optional)
- Fresh arugula (optional, for serving)

Let's get griddle-ing!

1. In a shallow dish, whisk together balsamic vinegar, olive oil, thyme, garlic powder, salt, and pepper.
2. Add portobello mushrooms to the marinade and coat them well. Marinate for at least 15 minutes, or up to 30 minutes for deeper flavor.
3. Preheat your griddle to medium-high heat. Remove mushrooms from the marinade and discard the marinade.
4. Grill portobello mushrooms for 5-7 minutes per side, or until tender and slightly charred.
5. Top with crumbled goat cheese (optional) and cook for an additional minute, if using, to melt the cheese.
6. Serve immediately on a bed of fresh arugula (optional)

Tips

- Marinate for bolder flavors.
- Brush leftover marinade on the griddle for extra oomph.
- Portobello crumbles can be used for vegetarian tacos or pasta.

Nutritional Information
(per serving)

Calories: 250, **Fat**: 15g,
Protein: 10g, **Carbs**: 20g

Turn to the mighty portobello for a hearty vegetarian main course! Marinated and grilled to juicy perfection, these mushroom steaks are a flavor explosion.

SPICY HARISSA CAULIFLOWER STEAKS WITH TAHINI SAUCE

Here's what you'll need

- 1 head of cauliflower, cut into 1-inch thick steaks
- 1/4 cup olive oil
- 2 tbsp harissa paste
- 1 tbsp lemon juice
- 1 tsp ground cumin
- 1/2 tsp salt
- 1/4 tsp black pepper

For the Tahini Sauce:
- 1/4 cup tahini paste
- 2 tbsp lemon juice
- 2 tbsp water
- 1 clove garlic, minced
- 1/4 cup chopped fresh parsley

SERVES 2

PREP TIME 10 mins

COOK TIME 15 mins

Let's get griddle-ing!

1. In a bowl, whisk together olive oil, harissa paste, lemon juice, cumin, salt, and pepper. Add cauliflower steaks and toss to coat.
2. Marinate cauliflower for at least 15 minutes, or up to 30 minutes for deeper flavor.
3. Preheat your griddle to medium heat. Grill cauliflower steaks for 5-7 minutes per side, or until tender and slightly charred.
4. While the cauliflower cooks, prepare the tahini sauce by whisking together tahini paste, lemon juice, water, garlic, and parsley.
5. Serve grilled cauliflower steaks drizzled with tahini sauce.

Tips
- Marinate for bolder flavors.
- Use a grill basket for easier flipping of cauliflower steaks.
- Leftover tahini sauce is great with veggies or pita bread.

Alex & Jamie
Blake

Nutritional Information
(per serving)

Calories: 200, **Fat**: 12g,
Protein: 4g, **Carbs**: 20g

Craving adventure? Spice up your griddle with harissa-marinated cauliflower steaks! Drizzled with a creamy tahini sauce, this dish is a flavor explosion for vegetarians and everyone else.

RAINBOW VEGGIE FAJITAS WITH GUACAMOLE

SERVES 4

PREP TIME 15 mins

COOK TIME 15 mins

Alex & Jamie
Blake

Here's what you'll need

- 1 bell pepper (any color), sliced
- 1 red onion, sliced
- 1 zucchini, sliced
- 1 yellow squash, sliced
- 1 cup broccoli florets
- 1/4 cup olive oil
- 2 tbsp fajita seasoning
- 1/2 lime, juiced
- 4 warmed tortillas
- Fresh cilantro (optional, for garnish)

For the Guacamole (optional):
- 1 ripe avocado, mashed
- 1/4 cup diced tomato
- 1 tbsp chopped red onion
- 1 tbsp lime juice
- 1/4 tsp salt

Let's get griddle-ing!

1. In a bowl, toss together bell peppers, onion, zucchini, yellow squash, and broccoli florets. Drizzle with olive oil, fajita seasoning, and lime juice.
2. Preheat your griddle to medium-high heat. Spread vegetables evenly on the preheated griddle.
3. Cook for 5-7 minutes per side, or until tender-crisp and slightly charred.
4. While the vegetables cook, prepare the guacamole (optional) by mashing avocado and combining it with diced tomato, red onion, lime juice, and salt. Garnish with fresh cilantro, if desired.
5. Serve fajita vegetables warm on tortillas with your prepared guacamole (optional) and your favorite fajita toppings like salsa, sour cream, and shredded cheese.

Tips

- Use a variety of colorful bell peppers for a visual feast!
- Grill leftover veggies for salads or wraps.
- Get creative with toppings! Try grilled pineapple or mango.

Nutritional Information
(per serving)

Calories: 300, **Fat:** 15g,
Protein: 5g, **Carbs:** 35g

Liven up your weeknight with a colorful veggie fajita fiesta! This customizable dish is packed with flavor and perfect for a fun, flame-kissed meal on your Blackstone.

VEGETARIAN BLACKSTONE BURGER WITH GRILLED VEGGIES

Here's what you'll need

- 1 veggie burger patty (store-bought or homemade)
- 1 hamburger bun
- Your favorite burger toppings (lettuce, tomato, cheese, etc.)

For the Grilled Veggies:
- 1/2 red onion, sliced
- 1/2 portobello mushroom, sliced
- 1/2 zucchini, sliced
- 1 tbsp olive oil
- 1/4 tsp salt
- 1/4 tsp black pepper

SERVES
1

PREP TIME
15 mins

COOK TIME
15 mins

Alex & Jamie
Blake

Let's get griddle-ing!

1. Preheat your griddle to medium heat. In a bowl, toss sliced onion, mushroom, and zucchini with olive oil, salt, and pepper.
2. Grill the burger patty and vegetables simultaneously on the preheated griddle. Cook the burger patty according to package instructions or desired doneness. Cook the vegetables for 3-4 minutes per side, or until tender-crisp and slightly charred.
3. Toast the hamburger bun on the griddle for a minute or two, if desired.
4. Assemble your burger with the patty, grilled vegetables, and your favorite toppings.

Tips

- Use a grill press to get nice grill marks on your burger patty.
- Experiment with different veggie combinations! Try grilled pineapple or bell peppers.
- Leftover grilled veggies can be added to salads or wraps..

Nutritional Information
(per serving)
Calories: 450, **Fat**: 20g,
Protein: 20g, **Carbs**: 40g

Craving a juicy burger but going meatless? Look no further than this veggie burger recipe for your Blackstone! It's customizable and oh-so-satisfying.

GRIDDLE-WRAPPED GOODNESS

HANDHELD DELIGHTS

Beyond the realm of sizzling steaks and fluffy pancakes lies a whole new world of possibilities on your Blackstone griddle: the realm of wraps, tacos, and sandwiches! This chapter delves into the magic of transforming simple ingredients into handheld masterpieces.

Here, the griddle steps up as a master of versatility, allowing you to create flavorful and convenient wraps, tacos bursting with fresh ingredients, and satisfying sandwiches toasted to crispy perfection.

Whether you're looking for a quick lunch option, a fun family dinner idea, or a portable meal for your next adventure, your Blackstone griddle has you covered.

So, grab your tortillas, break out the fillings, and get ready to experience the joy of creating delicious and satisfying wraps, tacos, and sandwiches, all on the sizzling surface of your Blackstone griddle!

Alex & Jamie
Blake

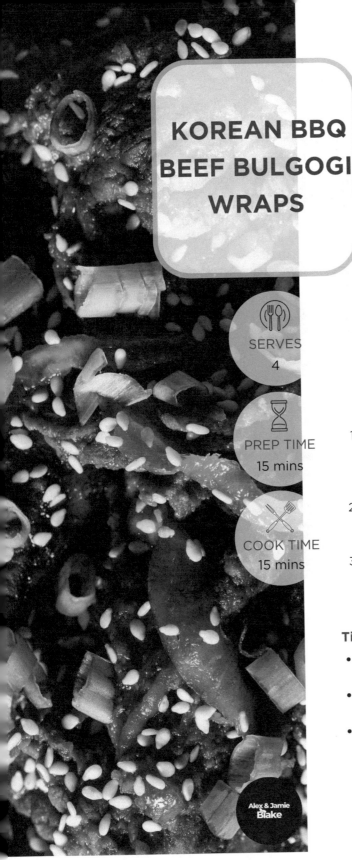

KOREAN BBQ BEEF BULGOGI WRAPS

SERVES
4

PREP TIME
15 mins

COOK TIME
15 mins

Alex & Jamie
Blake

Here's what you'll need

- 1 pound flank steak, thinly sliced
- 1/4 cup soy sauce
- 2 tbsp brown sugar
- 1 tbsp rice vinegar
- 1 tbsp sesame oil
- 1 tbsp grated ginger
- 1 clove garlic, minced
- 1/2 tsp sriracha
- Sesame seeds (optional, for garnish)
- Boston lettuce leaves
- Kimchi, chopped
- Gochujang sauce (optional)

Let's get griddle-ing!

1. In a bowl, whisk together soy sauce, brown sugar, rice vinegar, sesame oil, ginger, garlic, and sriracha to create a marinade. Add sliced beef and toss to coat. Marinate for at least 15 minutes, or up to 30 minutes for deeper flavor.
2. Preheat your griddle to medium-high heat. Sear the marinated beef for 3-4 minutes per side, or until cooked through.
3. To assemble wraps, place a few lettuce leaves on a plate. Add cooked beef, a dollop of kimchi, and a drizzle of gochujang sauce (optional) to each lettuce wrap. Garnish with sesame seeds (optional) and serve immediately.

Tips

- Use flank steak thinly sliced against the grain for maximum tenderness.
- For a spicier kick, add a pinch of red pepper flakes to the marinade.
- Leftover bulgogi can be served over rice bowls.

Nutritional Information
(per serving)

Calories: 400, **Fat**: 20g,
Protein: 30g, **Carbs**: 20g

A taste of Korea on your griddle! Marinated beef bulgogi with a touch of sweetness wrapped in lettuce leaves with kimchi and gochujang sauce

CALIFORNIA CHICKEN CAESAR WRAPS WITH GRILLED ROMAINE

SERVES
2

PREP TIME
15 mins

COOK TIME
10 mins

Alex & Jamie
Blake

Here's what you'll need

- 2 boneless, skinless chicken breasts
- 1 tbsp olive oil
- 1 tsp dried oregano
- 1/2 tsp salt
- 1/4 tsp black pepper
- 2 romaine hearts, halved lengthwise
- 1/4 cup Caesar dressing
- 2 whole wheat tortillas
- Shredded Parmesan cheese
- Chopped romaine lettuce (optional)

Let's get griddle-ing!

1. In a bowl, toss chicken breasts with olive oil, oregano, salt, and pepper.
2. Preheat your griddle to medium-high heat. Grill the chicken breasts for 5-7 minutes per side, or until cooked through.
3. While the chicken cooks, brush the cut sides of the romaine hearts with olive oil and place them cut-side down on the griddle for 1-2 minutes, or until lightly charred.
4. To assemble wraps, spread Caesar dressing on each tortilla. Layer with grilled romaine (charred side facing out), sliced chicken, Parmesan cheese, and chopped romaine lettuce (optional). Roll up tightly and serve immediately.

Tips

- Pound the chicken breasts to a thinner, more even thickness for quicker cooking.
- Use a grill press to get nice grill marks on the romaine hearts.
- Add other chopped vegetables like red onion or bell peppers for extra flavor.

Nutritional Information
(per serving)
Calories: 500, **Fat**: 25g,
Protein: 40g, **Carbs**: 30g

A taste of Korea on your griddle! Marinated beef bulgogi with a touch of sweetness wrapped in lettuce leaves with kimchi and gochujang sauce

BLACKSTONE PHILLY CHEESESTEAK

SERVES
2

PREP TIME
10 min

COOK TIME
10 mins

Alex & Jamie
Blake

Here's what you'll need

- 1 pound ribeye steak, thinly sliced
- 1 tbsp olive oil
- 1/2 onion, thinly sliced
- 2 hoagie rolls
- Provolone cheese slices (or cheese of your choice)
- Salt & pepper to taste

Let's get griddle-ing!

1. Preheat your griddle to medium-high heat. Toss sliced onions with a drizzle of olive oil.
2. Sear the steak slices for 2-3 minutes per side, or until desired doneness. Season with salt and pepper while cooking.
3. While the steak cooks, spread the onions on the griddle and cook for 3-4 minutes, or until softened and caramelized.
4. Toast the hoagie rolls on the griddle for a minute or two per side, until lightly browned and warm.
5. To assemble cheesesteaks, place steak slices on the bottom halves of the hoagie rolls. Top with caramelized onions and desired amount of cheese. Close the sandwiches and return them to the griddle for another minute or two, or until cheese is melted and gooey.

Tips

- Use leftover ribeye for fajitas, stir-fries, or salads.
- Get creative with the cheese! Try swiss cheese, cheddar cheese, or a cheese whiz spread.
- Serve with your favorite dipping sauce like horseradish or ketchup.

Nutritional Information
(per serving)

Calories: 700, **Fat**: 40g,
Protein: 50g, **Carbs**: 40g

A griddle classic! Thinly sliced ribeye steak with melty cheese and caramelized onions nestled in a toasted hoagie roll.

BLACK BEAN & CORN QUESADILLAS WITH CREAMY AVOCADO SAUCE

SERVES
2

PREP TIME
10 mins

COOK TIME
10 mins

Alex & Jamie
Blake

Here's what you'll need

- 1 can (15 oz) black beans, rinsed and drained
- 1/2 cup frozen corn
- 1/4 cup shredded cheese (cheddar, Monterey Jack, or your choice)
- 2 large flour tortillas
- For the Creamy Avocado Sauce:
- 1 ripe avocado, mashed
- 1/4 cup chopped fresh cilantro
- 1 tbsp lime juice
- 1/4 cup sour cream (optional)
- Salt & pepper to taste

Let's get griddle-ing!

1. In a bowl, combine black beans, corn, and shredded cheese.
2. Preheat your griddle to medium heat. Spread half of the black bean mixture onto one half of a flour tortilla. Fold the other half of the tortilla over to enclose the filling. Repeat with the second tortilla.
3. Grill the quesadillas for 2-3 minutes per side, or until golden brown and crispy.
4. While the quesadillas cook, prepare the avocado sauce by mashing the avocado with chopped cilantro, lime juice, sour cream (optional), salt, and pepper in a bowl.
5. Cut the quesadillas in half and serve with a dollop of creamy avocado sauce on the side.

Tips

- Add a pinch of chili powder or cumin to the black bean mixture for a smoky flavor.
- Use crumbled queso fresco cheese for a more authentic taste.
- Leftover quesadillas can be stored in the refrigerator and reheated in a pan or microwave.

Nutritional Information
(per serving)

Calories: 400, **Fat**: 20g,
Protein:15g, **Carbs**: 40g

A vegetarian twist on a classic! Black beans, corn, and melty cheese sandwiched between two crispy tortillas with a cool and creamy avocado sauce.

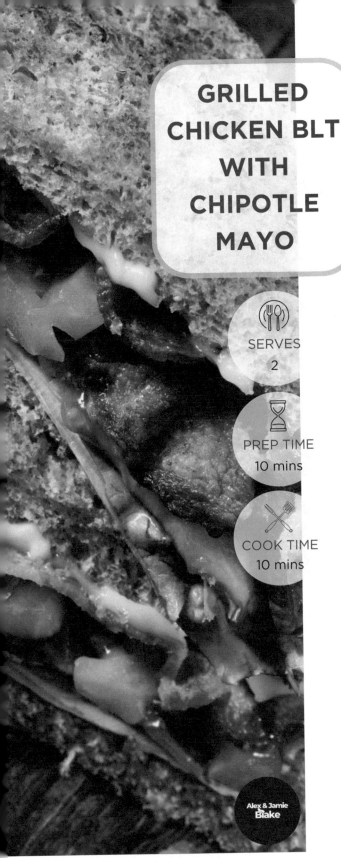

GRILLED CHICKEN BLT WITH CHIPOTLE MAYO

SERVES
2

PREP TIME
10 mins

COOK TIME
10 mins

Alex & Jamie
Blake

Here's what you'll need

- 1 boneless, skinless chicken breast
- 1 tbsp olive oil
- Salt & pepper to taste
- 2 slices bacon
- 2 slices toasted bread
- 2 lettuce leaves
- 1 tomato, sliced
- 1 tbsp mayonnaise
- 1/2 tsp chipotle pepper in adobo sauce, minced (optional)

Let's get griddle-ing!

1. Preheat your griddle to medium-high heat. Brush the chicken breast with olive oil and season with salt and pepper.
2. Grill the chicken breast for 5-7 minutes per side, or until cooked through.
3. While the chicken cooks, cook the bacon on the griddle for 5-7 minutes per side, or until crisp.
4. Toast the bread slices on the griddle for a minute or two per side, until lightly browned and warm.
5. In a small bowl, combine mayonnaise with minced chipotle pepper in adobo sauce (optional) to create a chipotle mayo.
6. To assemble the sandwich, spread chipotle mayo on one slice of toasted bread. Layer with lettuce, tomato, cooked bacon, and sliced chicken breast. Top with the other slice of toasted bread and serve immediately.

Tips

- Use leftover grilled chicken for salads or wraps.
- Get creative with the bread! Try sourdough bread, rye bread, or even a toasted bagel.
- For a spicier kick, add a few slices of jalapeno pepper to the sandwich.

Nutritional Information
(per serving)

Calories: 600, **Fat**: 35g,
Protein:40g, **Carbs**: 30g

A classic BLT gets a flavor upgrade with grilled chicken and a smoky chipotle mayo.

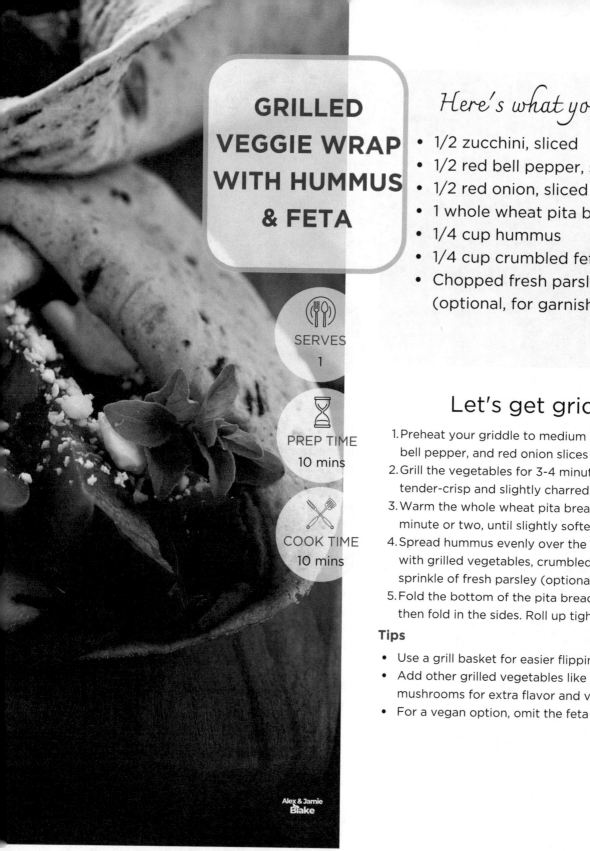

GRILLED VEGGIE WRAP WITH HUMMUS & FETA

SERVES 1

PREP TIME 10 mins

COOK TIME 10 mins

Here's what you'll need

- 1/2 zucchini, sliced
- 1/2 red bell pepper, sliced
- 1/2 red onion, sliced
- 1 whole wheat pita bread
- 1/4 cup hummus
- 1/4 cup crumbled feta cheese
- Chopped fresh parsley (optional, for garnish)

Let's get griddle-ing!

1. Preheat your griddle to medium heat. Brush the zucchini, bell pepper, and red onion slices with a little olive oil.
2. Grill the vegetables for 3-4 minutes per side, or until tender-crisp and slightly charred.
3. Warm the whole wheat pita bread on the griddle for a minute or two, until slightly softened and warmed through.
4. Spread hummus evenly over the warmed pita bread. Top with grilled vegetables, crumbled feta cheese, and a sprinkle of fresh parsley (optional).
5. Fold the bottom of the pita bread up and over the filling, then fold in the sides. Roll up tightly and serve immediately.

Tips

- Use a grill basket for easier flipping of the vegetables.
- Add other grilled vegetables like eggplant or portobello mushrooms for extra flavor and variety.
- For a vegan option, omit the feta cheese.

Alex & Jamie Blake

Nutritional Information
(per serving)

Calories: 400, **Fat:** 15g,
Protein: 10g, **Carbs:** 50g

A vegetarian delight packed with flavor and healthy goodness! Grilled vegetables, hummus, and crumbled feta cheese wrapped in a whole wheat pita bread.

BLACKSTONE S'MORES DESSERT QUESADILLA

SERVES
1

PREP TIME
5 mins

COOK TIME
5 mins

Alex & Jamie
Blake

Here's what you'll need

- 2 large marshmallows, halved
- 2 squares milk chocolate
- 1/4 cup graham cracker crumbs
- 1 large flour tortilla

Let's get griddle-ing!

1. Preheat your griddle to medium-low heat. Spread half of the graham cracker crumbs on one half of a flour tortilla. Top with chocolate squares and marshmallow halves.
2. Fold the other half of the tortilla over to enclose the filling.
3. Grill the quesadilla for 1-2 minutes per side, or until golden brown and the marshmallows are melted and gooey.
4. Cut the quesadilla in half and serve immediately while warm and gooey..

Tips

- Use a non-stick cooking spray to prevent sticking.
- For an extra decadent treat, add a drizzle of Nutella or peanut butter to the filling.
- Leftover s'mores quesadillas can be stored in the refrigerator and reheated in a pan or microwave, although the texture won't be quite the same

Nutritional Information
(per serving)

Calories: 400, **Fat**: 20g,
Protein:5g, **Carbs**: 50g

A fun and delicious twist on a classic dessert! Marshmallow, chocolate, and graham cracker crumbs sandwiched between two tortillas, creating a gooey and delightful treat on the griddle.

DIVE INTO DELICIOUSNESS
A SEAFOOD EXTRAVAGANZA ON THE BLACKSTONE GRIDDLE

Calling all seafood lovers! This chapter isn't just about flipping fish – it's about unlocking a world of sizzling sensations and ocean-fresh flavors on your trusty Blackstone griddle. Whether you're a seasoned grill master or just setting sail on your seafood grilling journey, we'll guide you through techniques that transform delicate scallops, succulent shrimp, and flaky fish into culinary masterpieces.

Forget about dry, overcooked seafood – here, we'll explore methods for achieving perfectly seared exteriors and juicy, tender interiors. So, grab your favorite catch and prepare to be amazed! This chapter is your gateway to griddle-licious seafood perfection, one delicious recipe at a time. Prepare to set sail on a culinary adventure where every bite is a taste of the ocean's bounty.

Alex & Jamie
Blake

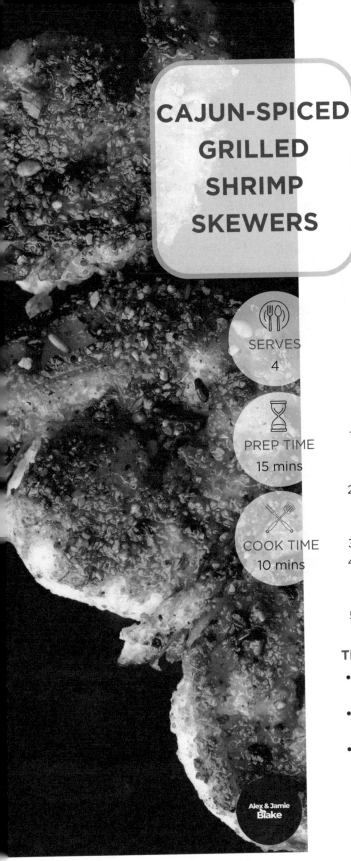

CAJUN-SPICED GRILLED SHRIMP SKEWERS

Here's what you'll need

- 1 pound large shrimp, peeled and deveined.
- 1 tbsp olive oil
- 1 tbsp Cajun seasoning
- 1/2 tsp smoked paprika
- 1/4 tsp garlic powder
- 1/4 tsp onion powder
- Salt & pepper to taste
- Wooden skewers

For Serving:
- Lemon wedges
- Cocktail sauce (optional)

SERVES
4

PREP TIME
15 mins

COOK TIME
10 mins

Let's get griddle-ing!

1. Preheat your griddle to medium-high heat. Soak wooden skewers in water for at least 30 minutes to prevent burning.
2. In a bowl, toss the shrimp with olive oil, Cajun seasoning, smoked paprika, garlic powder, onion powder, salt, and pepper.
3. Thread the shrimp onto the soaked wooden skewers.
4. Place the skewers on the preheated griddle and cook for 3-4 minutes per side, or until the shrimp are pink and opaque throughout.
5. Serve the Cajun-spiced grilled shrimp skewers hot with lemon wedges and cocktail sauce (optional) for dipping.

Tips

- Use jumbo shrimp for an even more impressive presentation.
- Customize the spice level by adjusting the amount of Cajun seasoning used.
- Leftover grilled shrimp can be used in salads, wraps, or tacos.

Alex & Jamie
Blake

Nutritional Information
(per serving)

Calories: 300, **Fat**: 15g,
Protein:30g, **Carbs**: 5g

These flavorful shrimp skewers are infused with a bold Cajun spice blend and perfect for a casual and delicious summer cookout.

HONEY GARLIC GLAZED SALMON FILLETS

SERVES
4

PREP TIME
10 mins

COOK TIME
15 mins

Alex & Jamie
Blake

Here's what you'll need

- 4 salmon fillets (around 6 oz each)
- 1 tbsp olive oil
- Salt & pepper to taste

For the Honey Garlic Glaze:
- 1/4 cup honey
- 2 tbsp soy sauce
- 1 tbsp sriracha (adjust to your spice preference)
- 1 tbsp grated ginger
- 1 clove garlic, minced

Let's get griddle-ing!

1. Preheat your griddle to medium heat.
2. Pat the salmon fillets dry with paper towels. Season them generously with salt and pepper.
3. In a small bowl, whisk together honey, soy sauce, sriracha, grated ginger, and minced garlic to create the honey garlic glaze.
4. Brush the salmon fillets with a thin layer of olive oil. Place them on the preheated griddle.
5. Cook the salmon for 5-7 minutes per side, or until cooked through and flaky.
6. In the last few minutes of cooking, brush the salmon fillets generously with the honey garlic glaze.
7. Serve the glazed salmon fillets immediately with your favorite sides.

Tips

- Use skin-on salmon fillets for added flavor and crispy skin.
- Marinate the salmon fillets in a mixture of soy sauce, brown sugar, and ginger for 30 minutes before grilling for extra depth of flavor.
- Leftover salmon can be flaked and used in salads, sandwiches, or fish cakes.

Nutritional Information
(per serving)
Calories: 400, **Fat**: 25g,
Protein:40g, **Carbs**: 10g

This simple yet flavorful recipe features salmon fillets glazed with a sweet and savory honey garlic sauce, perfect for a healthy and satisfying meal.

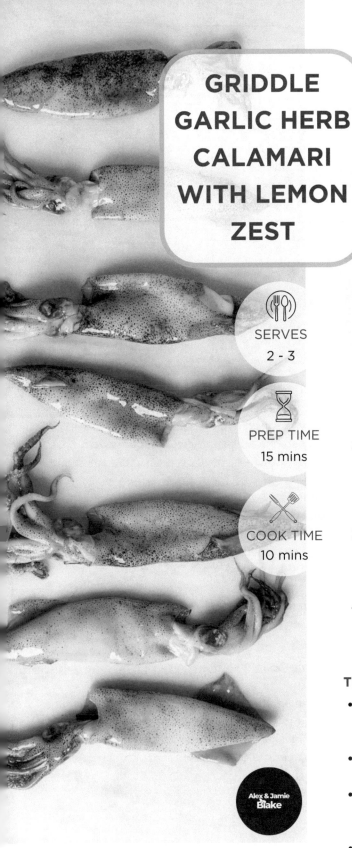

GRIDDLE GARLIC HERB CALAMARI WITH LEMON ZEST

SERVES
2 - 3

PREP TIME
15 mins

COOK TIME
10 mins

Alex & Jamie
Blake

Here's what you'll need

- 1 pound fresh calamari, cleaned and chopped into rings or tubes
- 2 tablespoons olive oil
- 2 cloves garlic, minced
- 1 tablespoon chopped fresh parsley
- 1/2 teaspoon dried oregano
- 1/4 teaspoon red pepper flakes (optional)
- Salt and freshly ground black pepper to taste
- 1 lemon, zested for garnish

Let's get griddle-ing!

1. Preheat your griddle to medium-high heat.
2. In a bowl, combine olive oil, minced garlic, chopped parsley, dried oregano, red pepper flakes (if using), salt, and pepper. Add the chopped calamari and toss to coat evenly. Marinate for at least 15 minutes, or up to 30 minutes for deeper flavor.
3. Spread the marinated calamari on the preheated griddle in a single layer. Cook for 2-3 minutes per side, or until the calamari becomes opaque and slightly browned. Be careful not to overcook, as calamari can become tough.
4. Remove the cooked calamari from the griddle and transfer it to a serving plate. Squeeze a bit of fresh lemon juice over the top (optional). Garnish generously with lemon zest for a bright citrusy finish.

Tips

- If you're not comfortable cleaning calamari yourself, ask your fishmonger to do it for you. The key is to remove the head, beak, and internal organs, then rinse thoroughly.
- Calamari cooks quickly. Don't overcook it, or it will become rubbery.
- This recipe is a great base. You can experiment with other herbs and spices in the marinade, such as thyme, paprika, or chili powder.
- Leftover calamari can be stored in an airtight container in the refrigerator for up to 2 days. Reheat gently in a pan or on the griddle until warmed through.

Nutritional Information (per serving)

Calories: 250, **Fat**: 15g,
Protein:30g, **Carbs**: 5g

This recipe transforms fresh calamari into a delightful griddle dish with a simple garlic herb marinade and a bright lemon zest topping.

BLACKENED MAHI-MAHI WITH CHIPOTLE CREMA

Here's what you'll need

- 4 mahi-mahi fillets (around 6 oz each)
- 1 tbsp olive oil
- 1 tbsp blackening seasoning
- Salt & pepper to taste

For the Chipotle Crema:
- 1/2 cup sour cream
- 1/4 cup mayonnaise
- 1 chipotle pepper in adobo sauce, chopped (adjust to your spice preference)
- 1 tbsp lime juice
- 1/4 tsp chopped fresh cilantro
- Salt & pepper to taste

SERVES
4

PREP TIME
10 mins

COOK TIME
15 mins

Let's get griddle-ing!

1. Preheat your griddle to medium-high heat.
2. Pat the mahi-mahi fillets dry with paper towels. Season them generously with olive oil, blackening seasoning, salt, and pepper.
3. In a separate bowl, whisk together sour cream, mayonnaise, chopped chipotle pepper, lime juice, chopped cilantro, salt, and pepper to create the chipotle crema.
4. Place the seasoned mahi-mahi fillets on the preheated griddle and cook for 3-4 minutes per side, or until cooked through and flaky.
5. Serve the blackened mahi-mahi fillets with a dollop of chipotle crema on top.

Tips

- Use a store-bought blackening seasoning for a quicker prep time.
- Adjust the amount of chipotle pepper in adobo sauce according to your desired spice level.
- Leftover blackened mahi-mahi can be served cold on a bed of salad greens or used in fish tacos.

Alex & Jamie
Blake

Nutritional Information
(per serving)

Calories: 500, **Fat:** 30g,
Protein: 40g, **Carbs:** 10g

This recipe features bold blackened seasoning on mahi-mahi fillets, balanced with a cool and creamy chipotle crema for a flavorful and satisfying main course.

CEDAR PLANK GRILLED SWORDFISH WITH LEMON DILL SAUCE

Here's what you'll need

- 4 swordfish steaks (around 6 oz each)
- 2 cedar planks, soaked in water for at least 30 minutes
- 1 tbsp olive oil
- Salt & pepper to taste

For the Lemon Dill Sauce:
- 1/2 cup mayonnaise
- 1/4 cup sour cream
- 1/4 cup chopped fresh dill
- 2 tbsp lemon juice
- 1 tsp Dijon mustard
- Salt & pepper to taste

SERVES
4

PREP TIME
30 mins

COOK TIME
20 mins

Alex & Jamie
Blake

Let's get griddle-ing!

1. Preheat your griddle to medium heat.
2. While the griddle preheats, soak the cedar planks in water for at least 30 minutes. Pat the swordfish steaks dry with paper towels. Season them lightly with olive oil, salt, and pepper.
3. In a separate bowl, whisk together mayonnaise, sour cream, chopped fresh dill, lemon juice, Dijon mustard, salt, and pepper to create the lemon dill sauce.
4. Place the soaked cedar planks directly on the preheated griddle. Once they begin to smoke (around 5 minutes), carefully place the seasoned swordfish steaks on top of the cedar planks.
5. Cover the griddle with a lid (optional) and cook the swordfish for 8-10 minutes per side, or until cooked through and flaky.
6. Serve the cedar plank-roasted swordfish with a dollop of lemon dill sauce on the side.

Tips

- Use a metal spatula to carefully flip the swordfish on the cedar plank.
- Substitute other fresh herbs like parsley or chives for dill in the sauce.
- Leftover swordfish can be flaked and used in fish cakes or chowder.

Nutritional Information
(per serving)

Calories: 450, **Fat**: 30g,
Protein:45g, **Carbs**: 5g

This recipe adds a touch of elegance to your griddle cooking with cedar plank-roasted swordfish infused with a smoky flavor and finished with a light and refreshing lemon dill sauce.

GARLIC BUTTER GRILLED LOBSTER TAILS

Here's what you'll need

- 2 whole lobster tails (8-10 oz each)
- 1 tbsp olive oil
- Salt & pepper to taste

For the Garlic Butter Sauce:

- 4 tbsp unsalted butter
- 2 cloves garlic, minced
- 1 tbsp fresh lemon juice
- 1/4 tsp chopped fresh parsley
- Salt & pepper to taste

SERVES
2

PREP TIME
10 mins

COOK TIME
15 mins

Alex & Jamie
Blake

Let's get griddle-ing!

1. Preheat your griddle to medium-high heat. Using kitchen shears, cut through the tough top shell of the lobster tails lengthwise, without severing the flesh completely.
2. Gently remove any vein running down the tail. Pat the lobster tails dry with paper towels. Season them generously with olive oil, salt, and pepper.
3. In a small saucepan, melt the butter over medium heat. Add minced garlic and cook for a minute, until fragrant. Stir in lemon juice, chopped parsley, salt, and pepper to create the garlic butter sauce.
4. Place the seasoned lobster tails flesh-side down on the preheated griddle. Cook for 3-4 minutes, or until the flesh becomes opaque.
5. Flip the lobster tails and brush them generously with the garlic butter sauce. Cook for an additional 2-3 minutes, or until the lobster is cooked through and the flesh is pearly white.
6. Serve the garlic butter grilled lobster tails immediately with any remaining garlic butter sauce for dipping.

Tips

- Ask your fishmonger to split and clean the lobster tails for you if needed.
- Use a meat thermometer to ensure the internal temperature of the thickest part of the lobster tail reaches 145°F (63°C) for safe consumption.
- Leftover lobster meat can be used in salads, pasta dishes, or lobster rolls.

Nutritional Information
(per serving)

Calories: 500, **Fat**: 35g,
Protein:40g, **Carbs**: 5g

Indulge in a luxurious meal with this recipe featuring simply seasoned lobster tails cooked to perfection on the griddle and finished with a decadent garlic butter sauce.

FISH TACOS WITH CILANTRO LIME CREMA

SERVES 4

PREP TIME 15 mins

COOK TIME 15 mins

Alex & Jamie Blake

Here's what you'll need

- 1 pound white fish fillets (cod, tilapia, or mahi-mahi)
- 1 tbsp olive oil
- 1 tbsp taco seasoning
- Salt & pepper to taste
- 4 corn tortillas, warmed
- Your favorite taco toppings (shredded cabbage, diced avocado, salsa, etc.)

For the Cilantro Lime Crema
- 1/2 cup sour cream
- 1/4 cup chopped fresh cilantro
- 1 tbsp lime juice
- 1/4 tsp garlic powder
- Salt & pepper to taste

Let's get griddle-ing!

1. Preheat your griddle to medium heat.
2. Cut the fish fillets into taco-sized pieces. In a bowl, toss the fish with olive oil, taco seasoning, salt, and pepper.
3. In a separate bowl, whisk together sour cream, chopped cilantro, lime juice, garlic powder, salt, and pepper to create the cilantro lime crema.
4. Place the fish pieces on the preheated griddle and cook for 3-4 minutes per side, or until cooked through and flaky.
5. Warm the corn tortillas on the griddle for a minute or two per side.
6. To assemble the tacos, fill the warmed tortillas with grilled fish, shredded cabbage, diced avocado, salsa, and a dollop of cilantro lime crema.

Tips
- Use pre-made taco seasoning for a quicker prep time.
- Get creative with the toppings! Try adding crumbled cheese, pickled onions, or a dollop of hot sauce.
- Leftover grilled fish can be used in salads, wraps, or fish cakes.

Nutritional Information (per serving)

Calories: 400, **Fat**: 20g, **Protein**:30g, **Carbs**: 30g

These light and flavorful tacos feature grilled fish, fresh toppings, and a creamy cilantro lime crema, perfect for a fun and casual family meal.

POULTRY TAKES FLIGHT ON THE GRIDDLE

GRIDDLE-SEARED PERFECTION FOR EVERY BIRD

Craving succulent chicken, juicy turkey, or flavorful duck? Look no further than your trusty Blackstone griddle! This chapter soars through a variety of poultry possibilities, showcasing the griddle's ability to transform these versatile proteins into mouthwatering masterpieces.

From smoky grilled chicken breasts to crispy-skinned duck confit, we'll explore techniques that unlock the full potential of your poultry.

Whether you're a seasoned grill master or a curious beginner, this chapter equips you with the knowledge and recipes to elevate your poultry game. So, get ready to unlock a world of deliciousness where your Blackstone griddle becomes the launchpad for unforgettable poultry dishes!

SPATCHCOCK CHICKEN WITH GRILLED LEMON & HERBS

SERVES
4

PREP TIME
15 mins

COOK TIME
45 mins

Alex & Jamie
Blake

Here's what you'll need

- 1 whole chicken (around 3-4 lbs)
- 1 tbsp olive oil
- 1 lemon, halved
- 4 sprigs fresh thyme
- 4 cloves garlic, smashed
- Salt & pepper to taste

Let's get griddle-ing!

1. Preheat your griddle to medium heat.
2. Spatchcock the Chicken: Using kitchen shears, remove the backbone of the chicken by cutting down either side of the spine. Flip the chicken breast-side up and press down firmly to flatten.
3. Brush the chicken with olive oil and season generously with salt and pepper. Tuck the lemon halves, thyme sprigs, and smashed garlic cloves under the skin of the chicken.
4. Place the chicken breast-side down on the preheated griddle. Cook for 30-35 minutes, or until the skin becomes golden brown and crispy.
5. Flip the chicken and cook for another 10-15 minutes, or until the internal temperature reaches 165°F (74°C) in the thickest part of the thigh.
6. Let the chicken rest for 10 minutes before carving and serving.

Tips

- Use kitchen twine to secure the spatchcocked chicken for even cooking.
- Substitute other herbs like rosemary or oregano for thyme.
- Leftover chicken can be used in salads, wraps, or sandwiches.

Nutritional Information (per serving)

Calories: 450, **Fat**: 30g,
Protein:50g, **Carbs**: 5g

A juicy and flavorful whole chicken roasted on the griddle, infused with the aroma of fresh lemon and herbs.

HONEY GARLIC GLAZED TURKEY BURGERS

SERVES 4

PREP TIME 15 mins

COOK TIME 15 mins

Alex & Jamie Blake

Here's what you'll need

- 1 pound ground turkey
- 1/4 cup panko breadcrumbs
- 1 tbsp soy sauce
- 1 tbsp honey
- 1 tbsp sriracha (adjust to your spice preference)
- 1 tbsp grated ginger
- 1 clove garlic, minced
- 1/4 cup chopped green onions
- Salt & pepper to taste
- Hamburger buns
- Your favorite burger toppings (lettuce, tomato, onion, cheese, etc.)

For the Honey Garlic Glaze:
- 2 tbsp soy sauce
- 1 tbsp honey
- 1 tbsp rice vinegar
- 1 clove garlic, minced

Let's get griddle-ing!

1. Preheat your griddle to medium-high heat.
2. In a large bowl, combine ground turkey, panko breadcrumbs, soy sauce, honey, sriracha, ginger, garlic, green onions, salt, and pepper. Mix well to combine.
3. Form the mixture into 4 equal patties.
4. Brush the patties with a thin layer of olive oil. Place them on the preheated griddle.
5. Cook the burgers for 5-7 minutes per side, or until cooked through and browned.
6. While the burgers cook, prepare the honey garlic glaze. In a small saucepan, whisk together soy sauce, honey, rice vinegar, and minced garlic. Bring to a simmer over medium heat and cook for 2-3 minutes, until slightly thickened.
7. Brush the cooked burgers with the honey garlic glaze in the last minute of cooking.
8. Serve the burgers on toasted hamburger buns with your favorite toppings.

Tips

- Use lean ground turkey for a healthier option.
- Get creative with the toppings! Try adding pineapple, avocado, or kimchi for a unique flavor twist.
- Leftover burgers can be stored in the refrigerator and reheated in a pan or microwave.

Nutritional Information
(per serving)
Calories: 450, **Fat:** 25g,
Protein: 40g, **Carbs:** 30g

A healthier twist on the classic burger, featuring ground turkey seasoned with Asian-inspired flavors.

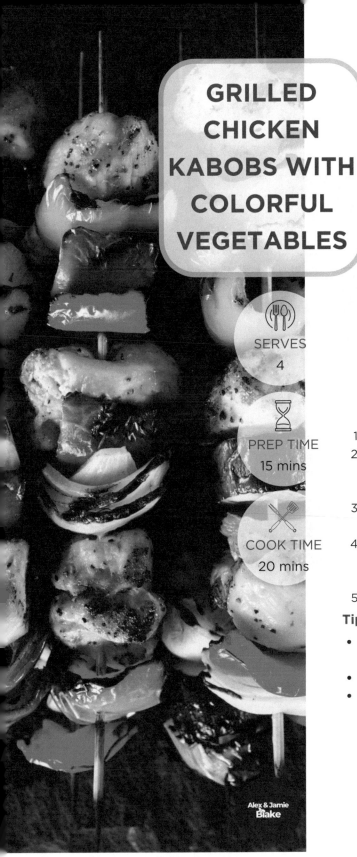

GRILLED CHICKEN KABOBS WITH COLORFUL VEGETABLES

SERVES
4

PREP TIME
15 mins

COOK TIME
20 mins

Here's what you'll need

- 1 pound boneless, skinless chicken breasts, cut into cubes
- 1 bell pepper (any color), cut into squares
- 1 red onion, cut into wedges
- 1 zucchini, cut into chunks
- 1 yellow squash, cut into chunks
- 1/4 cup olive oil
- 1 tbsp Italian seasoning
- 1/2 tsp salt
- 1/4 tsp black pepper
- Wooden skewers

Let's get griddle-ing!

1. Preheat your griddle to medium-high heat.
2. In a bowl, toss the chicken cubes, bell pepper squares, red onion wedges, zucchini chunks, and yellow squash chunks with olive oil, Italian seasoning, salt, and pepper.
3. Thread the vegetables and chicken cubes onto wooden skewers, alternating ingredients for colorful presentation.
4. Place the skewers on the preheated griddle. Cook for 10-15 minutes per side, or until the chicken is cooked through and the vegetables are tender-crisp.
5. Serve the kabobs hot with your favorite dipping sauce.

Tips

- Soak the wooden skewers in water for at least 30 minutes before grilling to prevent burning.
- Use pre-cut vegetables for quicker prep time.
- Leftover grilled chicken and vegetables can be used in salads, wraps, or bowls.

Alex & Jamie Blake

Nutritional Information
(per serving)

Calories: 400, **Fat**: 20g,
Protein:30g, **Carbs**: 25g

A fun and healthy way to grill chicken and vegetables, perfect for a summer cookout.

TANDOORI CHICKEN NAAN PIZZAS

SERVES 2

PREP TIME 10 mins

COOK TIME 15 mins

Alex & Jamie
Blake

Here's what you'll need

- 2 boneless, skinless chicken thighs, thinly sliced
- 1/4 cup plain yogurt
- 1 tbsp tandoori masala powder
- 1 tbsp lemon juice
- 1/2 tsp ginger paste
- 1/4 tsp garlic paste
- 1/4 tsp garam masala powder
- Salt & pepper to taste
- 2 large naan breads
- 1/2 cup shredded mozzarella cheese
- 1/4 cup chopped red onion
- 1/4 cup chopped green bell pepper
- Chopped fresh cilantro (optional, for garnish)

Let's get griddle-ing!

1. In a bowl, combine yogurt, tandoori masala powder, lemon juice, ginger paste, garlic paste, garam masala powder, salt, and pepper to create a marinade. Add sliced chicken thighs and toss to coat. Marinate for at least 15 minutes, or up to 30 minutes for deeper flavor.
2. Preheat your griddle to medium heat.
3. Grill the marinated chicken slices for 3-4 minutes per side, or until cooked through.
4. While the chicken cooks, warm the naan breads on the griddle for a minute or two per side, until slightly softened and warmed through.
5. Spread a thin layer of leftover marinade on each warmed naan bread (optional). Top with shredded mozzarella cheese, chopped red onion, chopped green bell pepper, and cooked tandoori chicken slices.
6. Return the naan pizzas to the griddle and cook for 2-3 minutes, or until the cheese is melted and bubbly.
7. Garnish with chopped fresh cilantro (optional) and serve immediately.

Tips

- Use store-bought tandoori masala paste for a quicker marinade.
- Get creative with the toppings! Try adding chopped mango, sliced cucumber, or a drizzle of raita sauce for a refreshing touch.
- Leftover tandoori chicken can be used in salads, wraps, or bowls.

Nutritional Information
(per serving)

Calories: 500, **Fat**: 25g,
Protein:40g, **Carbs**: 40g

A unique fusion of Indian flavors with a fun pizza twist! Perfect for a quick and satisfying meal.

LEMON PEPPER CHICKEN WITH GRILLED ASPARAGUS

Here's what you'll need

- 2 boneless, skinless chicken breasts
- 1 tbsp olive oil
- 1 tbsp lemon pepper seasoning
- 1 bunch asparagus, trimmed
- Salt & pepper to taste

SERVES 2

PREP TIME 10 mins

COOK TIME 15 mins

Let's get griddle-ing!

1. Preheat your griddle to medium heat.
2. Brush the chicken breasts with olive oil and season generously with lemon pepper seasoning.
3. Place the chicken breasts on the preheated griddle. Cook for 7-8 minutes per side, or until cooked through and the juices run clear.
4. While the chicken cooks, toss the asparagus spears with a drizzle of olive oil, salt, and pepper.
5. Add the asparagus to the griddle in the last 5 minutes of cooking the chicken. Cook the asparagus until tender-crisp, turning occasionally.
6. Serve the grilled chicken breasts with the asparagus.

Tips

- Marinate the chicken breasts in lemon juice and olive oil for 30 minutes before grilling for extra flavor.
- Grill cherry tomatoes or other vegetables alongside the asparagus for a more colorful plate.
- Leftover chicken can be used in salads, wraps, or sandwiches.

Alex & Jamie Blake

Nutritional Information (per serving)

Calories: 350, **Fat**: 20g, **Protein**:40g, **Carbs**: 5g

A simple and light dish featuring juicy chicken seasoned with lemon and pepper, paired with tender grilled asparagus.

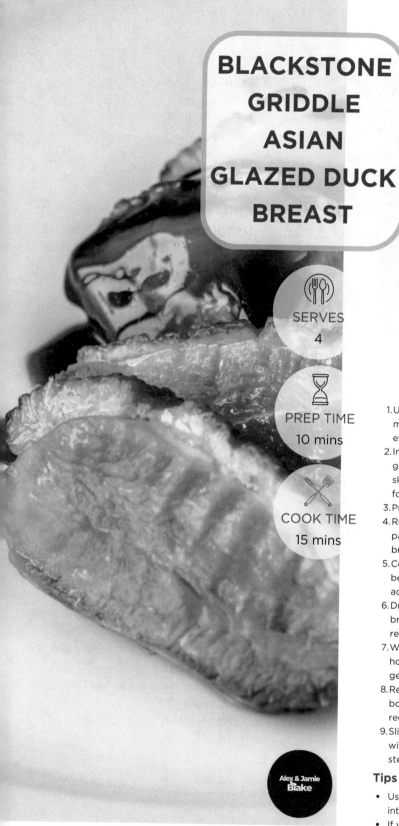

BLACKSTONE GRIDDLE ASIAN GLAZED DUCK BREAST

SERVES
4

PREP TIME
10 mins

COOK TIME
15 mins

Alex & Jamie
Blake

Here's what you'll need

- 2 duck breasts (skin-on)
- 1 tablespoon soy sauce
- 1 tablespoon rice vinegar
- 1 tablespoon honey
- 1 tablespoon hoisin sauce
- 1 teaspoon Sriracha (adjust for desired spice level)
- 1 clove garlic, minced
- 1 teaspoon grated ginger
- 1/2 teaspoon sesame oil
- Salt and freshly ground black pepper

Let's get griddle-ing!

1. Using a sharp knife, score the duck skin diagonally in a crisscross pattern, making sure not to cut through the flesh. This allows the fat to render more effectively and creates a crispy texture.
2. In a bowl, combine soy sauce, rice vinegar, hoisin sauce, Sriracha, garlic, ginger, and sesame oil. Whisk well. Place the duck breasts in the marinade, skin side up, and cover. Refrigerate for at least 30 minutes, or up to 4 hours for deeper flavor.
3. Preheat your Blackstone griddle to medium-high heat (around 400°F).
4. Remove the duck breasts from the marinade (if using) and pat them dry with paper towels. Season generously with salt and pepper. Place the duck breasts, skin-side down, on the preheated griddle.
5. Cook for 5-7 minutes without moving, allowing the skin to render and become crispy. You should see golden brown, crispy skin and some fat accumulating on the griddle.
6. Drain off some of the excess fat from the griddle if needed. Flip the duck breasts and cook for another 3-4 minutes, or until the internal temperature reaches 160°F for medium-rare (adjust cooking time for desired doneness).
7. While the duck breasts are cooking on the second side, whisk together the honey in a small bowl. In the last minute of cooking, brush the honey glaze generously over the duck skin. Let it caramelize slightly for extra flavor.
8. Remove the duck breasts from the griddle and transfer them to a cutting board. Tent with foil and let them rest for 5-10 minutes to allow the juices to redistribute. This ensures a more tender and flavorful bite.
9. Slice the duck breasts thinly against the grain and serve immediately. Drizzle with any remaining pan drippings or glaze. The duck breast pairs well with steamed rice, stir-fried vegetables, or a simple salad with a light vinaigrette.

Tips

- Use a meat thermometer to ensure the duck breasts reach the desired internal temperature for food safety.
- If you don't have Sriracha, you can substitute it with another chili sauce or red pepper flakes for a touch of heat.
- You can adjust the amount of Sriracha in the glaze to suit your spice preference.
- Leftover duck breast can be stored in an airtight container in the refrigerator for up to 3 days. Reheat gently on the griddle or in a pan until warmed through.

Nutritional Information
(per serving)

Calories: 500, **Fat**: 35g,
Protein:30g, **Carbs**: 10g

This recipe takes advantage of the Blackstone griddle's ability to achieve a beautiful sear while infusing the duck breast with smoky flavors. The Asian glaze adds a sweet and savory twist, making this dish perfect for a flavorful and impressive meal.

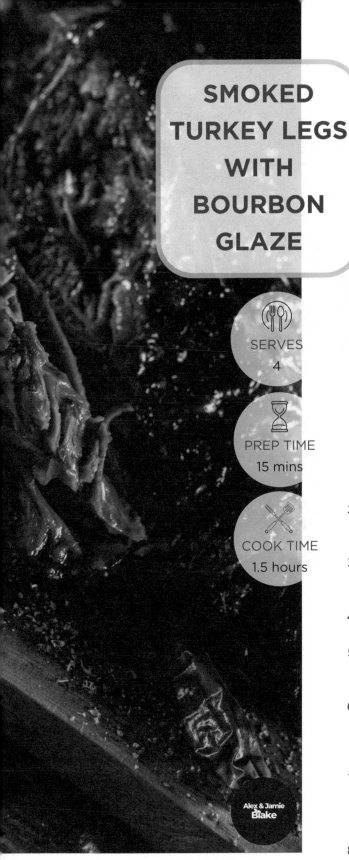

SMOKED TURKEY LEGS WITH BOURBON GLAZE

SERVES
4

PREP TIME
15 mins

COOK TIME
1.5 hours

Alex & Jamie
Blake

Here's what you'll need

- 4 whole turkey legs (around 1.5-2 lbs each)
- 1 tbsp olive oil
- 1 tbsp smoked paprika
- 1 tsp garlic powder
- 1/2 tsp onion powder
- 1/4 tsp black pepper
- 1 cup chicken broth
- 1/2 cup bourbon (optional, substitute with apple juice for a non-alcoholic version)
- 1/4 cup brown sugar
- 1 tbsp Dijon mustard
- Wood chips for smoking (optional)

Let's get griddle-ing!

1. Preheat your griddle to medium heat. If using wood chips for smoking, preheat a smoker box according to the manufacturer's instructions and place it on the preheated griddle.
2. Pat the turkey legs dry with paper towels. In a bowl, toss the turkey legs with olive oil, smoked paprika, garlic powder, onion powder, and black pepper.
3. Place the turkey legs on the preheated griddle, skin side down. If using wood chips, add them to the smoker box according to the manufacturer's instructions for smoking.
4. Pour the chicken broth around the turkey legs to prevent them from drying out.
5. Cover the griddle with aluminum foil to create an indirect heat environment. Reduce heat to medium-low and cook for 1 hour, flipping the turkey legs halfway through cooking.
6. In a small saucepan, whisk together bourbon (or apple juice), brown sugar, and Dijon mustard to create a glaze. Bring to a simmer over medium heat and cook for 5 minutes, or until slightly thickened.
7. In the last 15 minutes of cooking, brush the turkey legs generously with the bourbon glaze. Continue cooking until the internal temperature of the thickest part of the turkey leg reaches 165°F (74°C).
8. Serve the smoked turkey legs hot with your favorite barbecue sauce or dipping sauce.

Tips

- Use a meat thermometer to ensure the turkey legs are cooked through to a safe internal temperature.
- Marinate the turkey legs overnight for extra flavor.
- Leftover smoked turkey can be used in salads, sandwiches, or wraps.

Nutritional Information
(per serving)

Calories: 500, **Fat**: 30g, **Protein**:45g, **Carbs**: 20g

A crowd-pleasing recipe perfect for a backyard barbecue, featuring smoky turkey legs and a sweet and savory bourbon glaze.

OINK YOUR WAY TO FLAVORTOWN

A PORK PARADISE ON THE BLACKSTONE GRIDDLE

Calling all pork aficionados! This chapter isn't just about sizzling bacon – it's a celebration of the incredible versatility of pork on your trusty Blackstone griddle. From succulent chops and juicy tenderloin to flavorful ribs and smoky pulled pork, we'll transform this classic protein into a symphony of deliciousness.

Whether you're a seasoned grill master or a curious carnivore just starting your pork journey, we've got you covered. We'll delve into techniques that unlock the full potential of every cut, ensuring perfectly cooked, tender, and bursting-with-flavor results.

So, fire up your griddle, grab your favorite cut of pork, and get ready to experience a world of flavor. This chapter is your gateway to griddle-licious pork perfection, one delicious recipe at a time. Prepare to oink your way to flavortown with every bite!

Alex & Jamie Blake

SEARED PORK CHOPS WITH HERB BUTTER AND CRISPY APPLES

SERVES
2

PREP TIME
15 mins

COOK TIME
15 mins

Alex & Jamie
Blake

Here's what you'll need

- 2 bone-in pork loin chops (1-inch thick)
- 1 tbsp olive oil
- Salt & pepper to taste
- 1 apple, sliced

For the Herb Butter:
- 4 tbsp unsalted butter, softened
- 1 tbsp chopped fresh parsley
- 1 tbsp chopped fresh thyme
- 1 clove garlic, minced
- Salt & pepper to taste

Let's get griddle-ing!

1. Preheat your griddle to medium-high heat. Pat the pork chops dry with paper towels. Season generously with olive oil, salt, and pepper.
2. In a small bowl, combine softened butter, chopped parsley, chopped thyme, minced garlic, salt, and pepper to create the herb butter.
3. Place the seasoned pork chops on the preheated griddle. Cook for 4-5 minutes per side for medium-rare, or until desired doneness.
4. While the pork chops cook, melt a pat of butter on the griddle next to the chops. Add the sliced apples and cook for 2-3 minutes per side, or until softened and slightly caramelized.
5. Remove the cooked pork chops and apples from the griddle.
6. Spoon the herb butter over the pork chops and serve immediately

Tips

- Ask your butcher to French-trim the pork chops for a cleaner presentation.
- Use a meat thermometer to ensure the internal temperature of the pork chops reaches 145°F (medium-rare).
- Substitute fresh rosemary or chives for parsley and thyme in the herb butter.
- Leftover pork chops can be sliced and used in salads or wraps.

Nutritional Information
(per serving)

Calories: 650, **Fat**: 45g,
Protein:50g, **Carbs**: 20g

This classic recipe features perfectly seared pork chops topped with a decadent herb butter and served with a touch of sweetness from pan-fried apples.

HONEY GARLIC GLAZED PORK TENDERLOIN WITH GRILLED PINEAPPLE

Here's what you'll need

- 1 pork tenderloin (1-1.5 pounds)
- 1 tbsp olive oil
- Salt & pepper to taste
- 1 pineapple, cut into rings (optional)

For the Honey Garlic Glaze:
- 1/4 cup honey
- 2 tbsp soy sauce
- 1 tbsp brown sugar
- 1 tbsp Dijon mustard
- 1 tbsp rice vinegar
- 1 clove garlic, minced

SERVES
4

PREP TIME
10 mins

COOK TIME
20 mins

Alex & Jamie
Blake

Let's get griddle-ing!

1. Preheat your griddle to medium heat. Pat the pork tenderloin dry with paper towels. Season generously with olive oil, salt, and pepper.
2. In a small bowl, whisk together honey, soy sauce, brown sugar, Dijon mustard, rice vinegar, and minced garlic to create the honey garlic glaze.
3. Place the seasoned pork tenderloin on the preheated griddle. Cook for 15-20 minutes, turning occasionally, until the internal temperature reaches 145°F (medium-rare). Baste the pork tenderloin with the honey garlic glaze during the last few minutes of cooking.
4. If using pineapple, brush the slices with melted butter and grill them on the griddle for a minute or two per side, until slightly caramelized.
5. Remove the cooked pork tenderloin and pineapple (if using) from the griddle. Let the pork rest for a few minutes before slicing.
6. Serve the sliced pork tenderloin with the honey garlic glaze and grilled pineapple slices (optional).

Tips

- Marinate the pork tenderloin in the honey garlic glaze for 30 minutes before cooking for extra flavor.
- Substitute fresh ginger for the garlic in the glaze if desired.
- Serve the pork tenderloin with steamed vegetables or rice

Nutritional Information
(per serving)

Calories: 400, **Fat:** 25g,
Protein: 45g, **Carbs:** 20g

This recipe features a flavorful pork tenderloin glazed with a sweet and savory honey garlic sauce, served alongside grilled pineapple slices for a tropical twist.

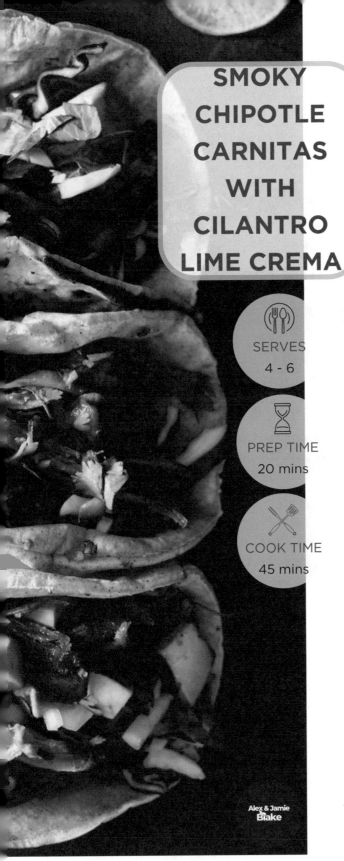

SMOKY CHIPOTLE CARNITAS WITH CILANTRO LIME CREMA

SERVES
4 - 6

PREP TIME
20 mins

COOK TIME
45 mins

Alex & Jamie
Blake

Here's what you'll need

- 2-3 pounds boneless pork shoulder
- 1 tbsp olive oil
- Salt & pepper to taste
- Corn tortillas (for serving)

For the Cilantro Lime Crema:

- 1 cup sour cream
- 1/4 cup chopped fresh cilantro
- 1 tbsp lime juice
- Salt & pepper to taste

For the Chipotle Marinade:

- 2 tbsp chipotle peppers in adobo sauce, chopped
- 1/4 cup orange juice
- 2 tbsp lime juice
- 1 tbsp soy sauce
- 1 tsp ground cumin
- 1/2 tsp chili powder
- 1/4 tsp smoked paprika
- 1 clove garlic, minced

Let's get griddle-ing!

1. Preheat your griddle to low (around 225°F) if it has a low setting. If not, use a smoker box filled with wood chips to create smoke.
2. In a bowl, combine chopped chipotle peppers in adobo sauce, orange juice, lime juice, soy sauce, ground cumin, chili powder, smoked paprika, and minced garlic to create the chipotle marinade.
3. Cut the pork shoulder into 2-3 inch cubes and place them in a large resealable bag. Pour the chipotle marinade over the pork and toss to coat evenly. Marinate for at least 30 minutes, or up to overnight for deeper flavor.
4. Remove the pork cubes from the marinade and pat them dry with paper towels. Season generously with olive oil, salt, and pepper.
5. Place the seasoned pork cubes on the preheated griddle. If using a smoker box, add wood chips according to the manufacturer's instructions.
6. Smoke the pork cubes for 45 minutes to 1 hour, or until the internal temperature reaches 190°F (for pulling). Shred the pork with two forks while it's hot.
7. While the pork smokes, prepare the cilantro lime crema by whisking together sour cream, chopped fresh cilantro, lime juice, salt, and pepper in a bowl.
8. Serve the smoky chipotle pork carnitas on corn tortillas with a dollop of cilantro lime crema and your favorite toppings like chopped onion, cilantro, and avocado.

Tips

- Use a meat thermometer to ensure the internal temperature of the pork reaches 190°F for shredding.
- Adjust the amount of chipotle peppers in the marinade according to your preference for heat.
- Serve the pork carnitas with other toppings like shredded cheese, salsa, and pickled jalapenos.
- Leftover carnitas can be used in burritos, tacos, or breakfast scrambles.

Nutritional Information
(per serving)

Calories: 500, **Fat**: 30g,
Protein:40g, **Carbs**: 25g

This recipe transforms your Blackstone griddle into a smoker, creating tender and flavorful pulled pork infused with smoky chipotle chilies. Serve with a refreshing cilantro lime crema for a taste of Mexico

SIZZLING KOREAN BBQ PORK BELLY WITH SPICY GOCHUJANG GLAZE

SERVES 2 - 3

PREP TIME 15 mins

COOK TIME 10 mins

Alex & Jamie Blake

Here's what you'll need

- 1 pound pork belly, thinly sliced
- 1 tbsp soy sauce
- 1 tbsp brown sugar
- 1 tbsp rice vinegar
- 1 tbsp gochujang (Korean chili paste)
- 1 tsp sesame oil
- 1 clove garlic, minced
- 1/2 tsp grated ginger
- Salt & pepper to taste
- Sesame seeds (for garnish, optional)

Let's get griddle-ing!

1. In a bowl, whisk together soy sauce, brown sugar, rice vinegar, gochujang, sesame oil, minced garlic, grated ginger, salt, and pepper to create the gochujang glaze.
2. Place the thinly sliced pork belly in a shallow dish and add the gochujang glaze. Toss to coat evenly and marinate for at least 15 minutes.
3. Preheat your griddle to medium-high heat.
4. Remove the pork belly slices from the marinade and shake off any excess.
5. Place the pork belly slices on the preheated griddle and cook for 3-4 minutes per side, or until browned and crispy.
6. Serve the sizzling Korean BBQ pork belly immediately with additional gochujang glaze for dipping (optional) and garnish with sesame seeds (optional). Enjoy wrapped in lettuce leaves with your favorite banchan (Korean side dishes).

Tips

- Ask your butcher to thinly slice the pork belly for easier cooking.
- You can adjust the amount of gochujang in the marinade according to your preference for heat.
- Substitute sriracha for gochujang if desired, but note that the flavor profile will be slightly different.
- Serve the Korean BBQ pork belly with kimchi, pickled vegetables, and steamed rice.
- Leftover pork belly can be used in fried rice dishes or lettuce wraps.

Nutritional Information (per serving)

Calories: 500, **Fat**: 40g, **Protein**:30g, **Carbs**: 20g

This recipe features thinly sliced pork belly marinated in a sweet and spicy Korean gochujang sauce and then cooked to crispy perfection on your Blackstone griddle.

JUICY BACON-WRAPPED PORK MEDALLIONS WITH CREAMY DIJON SAUCE

SERVES 4

PREP TIME 15 mins

COOK TIME 10 mins

Alex & Jamie
Blake

Here's what you'll need

- 1 pound pork tenderloin, cut into 1-inch thick medallions
- 8 slices thin bacon
- 1 tbsp olive oil
- Salt & pepper to taste

For the Creamy Dijon Sauce:
- 1/2 cup mayonnaise
- 2 tbsp Dijon mustard
- 1 tbsp heavy cream
- 1 tbsp chopped fresh parsley
- 1 tsp lemon juice
- Salt & pepper to taste

Let's get griddle-ing!

1. Preheat your griddle to medium-high heat. Pat the pork medallions dry with paper towels. Season generously with olive oil, salt, and pepper.
2. Wrap each pork medallion with a slice of bacon, securing it with a toothpick if needed.
3. In a small bowl, whisk together mayonnaise, Dijon mustard, heavy cream, chopped fresh parsley, lemon juice, salt, and pepper to create the creamy Dijon sauce.
4. Place the bacon-wrapped pork medallions on the preheated griddle. Cook for 4-5 minutes per side, or until the bacon is crispy and the pork is cooked through (internal temperature of 145°F for medium-rare).
5. Remove the cooked pork medallions from the griddle and let them rest for a few minutes before serving.
6. Warm the creamy Dijon sauce in a small saucepan over low heat until slightly warmed through (optional).
7. Serve the juicy bacon-wrapped pork medallions drizzled with the creamy Dijon sauce.

Tips
- Ask your butcher to cut the pork tenderloin into medallions of even thickness for consistent cooking.
- Substitute prosciutto or pancetta for bacon if desired.
- Use a meat thermometer to ensure the internal temperature of the pork reaches 145°F for medium-rare.
- Serve the bacon-wrapped pork medallions with mashed potatoes, roasted vegetables, or a side salad.
- Leftovers can be sliced and used in sandwiches or wraps.

Nutritional Information (per serving)

Calories: 550, **Fat**: 40g, **Protein**:45g, **Carbs**: 5g

This recipe features tender pork medallions wrapped in crispy bacon and cooked to perfection on the griddle. A creamy Dijon sauce adds a touch of elegance to this simple yet satisfying dish.

CRISPY PORK SCHNITZEL WITH CREAMY LEMON DILL SAUCE

SERVES
4

PREP TIME
15 mins

COOK TIME
10 mins

Alex & Jamie
Blake

Here's what you'll need

- 4 boneless pork loin chops (cut thin, about 1/2-inch thick)
- 1 cup all-purpose flour
- 2 large eggs, beaten
- 1 cup panko breadcrumbs
- Salt & pepper to taste
- Vegetable oil

For the Creamy Lemon Dill Sauce:
- 1/2 cup mayonnaise
- 1/4 cup sour cream
- 1 tbsp lemon juice
- 1 tbsp chopped fresh dill
- Salt & pepper to taste

Let's get griddle-ing!

1. Preheat your griddle to medium-high heat.
2. Pound the pork loin chops between two sheets of plastic wrap to an even thickness of about 1/2 inch.
3. Set up a breading station with three shallow dishes: one with flour seasoned with salt and pepper, one with beaten eggs, and one with panko breadcrumbs.
4. Dredge each pork chop in the flour, then dip it in the beaten eggs, and finally coat it evenly with panko breadcrumbs.
5. Add enough vegetable oil to lightly coat the bottom of the preheated griddle.
6. Carefully place the breaded pork chops on the griddle. Cook for 3-4 minutes per side, or until golden brown and cooked through.
7. While the pork chops cook, prepare the creamy lemon dill sauce by whisking together mayonnaise, sour cream, lemon juice, chopped fresh dill, salt, and pepper in a small bowl.
8. Serve the crispy pork schnitzel hot with the creamy lemon dill sauce for dipping.

Tips

- Use a meat mallet to pound the pork chops if you don't have a meat pounder.
- Substitute crushed crackers or cornflakes for the panko breadcrumbs if desired.
- Serve the pork schnitzel with mashed potatoes, roasted vegetables, or a side salad.
- Leftovers can be stored in the refrigerator for up to 3 days and reheated in a pan or oven.

Nutritional Information (per serving)

Calories: 500, **Fat**: 30g, **Protein**:40g, **Carbs**: 30g

This recipe features a classic German dish of breaded and pan-fried pork cutlets served with a refreshing lemon dill sauce. Your Blackstone griddle provides the perfect platform for achieving a satisfyingly crispy crust.

PULLED PORK NACHOS WITH SPICY PINEAPPLE SALSA

SERVES
4 - 6

PREP TIME
20 mins

COOK TIME
45 mins

Alex & Jamie
Blake

Here's what you'll need

- 2-3 pounds boneless pork shoulder
- 1 tbsp olive oil
- Salt & pepper to taste
- Tortilla chips (for serving)
- Shredded cheese (optional)
- Sour cream (optional)
- Guacamole (optional)

For the Spicy Pineapple Salsa
- 1 ripe pineapple, chopped
- 1 jalapeno pepper, seeded and chopped (adjust to your spice preference)
- 1/4 cup red onion, chopped
- 1 tbsp chopped fresh cilantro
- 1 tbsp lime juice
- Salt & pepper to taste

For the Chipotle Marinade
- 2 tbsp chipotle peppers in adobo sauce, chopped
- 1/4 cup orange juice
- 2 tbsp lime juice
- 1 tbsp soy sauce
- 1 tsp ground cumin
- 1/2 tsp chili powder
- 1/4 tsp smoked paprika
- 1 clove garlic, minced

Let's get griddle-ing!

1. Preheat your griddle to low (around 225°F) if it has a low setting. If not, use a smoker box filled with wood chips to create smoke.
2. In a bowl, combine chopped chipotle peppers in adobo sauce, orange juice, lime juice, soy sauce, ground cumin, chili powder, smoked paprika, and minced garlic to create the chipotle marinade.
3. Cut the pork shoulder into 2-3 inch cubes and place them in a large resealable bag. Pour the chipotle marinade over the pork and toss to coat evenly. Marinate for at least 30 minutes, or up to overnight for deeper flavor.
4. Remove the pork cubes from the marinade and pat them dry with paper towels.
5. Season generously with olive oil, salt, and pepper.
6. Place the seasoned pork cubes on the preheated griddle. If using a smoker box, add wood chips according to the manufacturer's instructions.
7. Smoke the pork cubes for 45 minutes to 1 hour, or until the internal temperature reaches 190°F (for pulling). Shred the pork with two forks while it's hot.
8. While the pork smokes, prepare the spicy pineapple salsa by combining chopped pineapple, jalapeno pepper, red onion, chopped fresh cilantro, lime juice, salt, and pepper in a bowl. Adjust the amount of jalapeno for your desired spice level.
9. To assemble the nachos, spread a layer of tortilla chips on a large platter or baking sheet. Top with shredded pulled pork, your favorite shredded cheese (optional), and a dollop of sour cream and guacamole (optional).
10. Heat the assembled nachos under a broiler for a few minutes until the cheese is melted and bubbly (optional).
11. Drizzle the spicy pineapple salsa over the loaded nachos and serve immediately. Enjoy the smoky pulled pork, the refreshing sweetness of the pineapple salsa, and the contrasting textures of the chips and cheese for a truly delicious experience!

Tips

- Use a meat thermometer to ensure the internal temperature of the pork reaches 190°F for shredding.
- Substitute other fruits like mango or peaches for the pineapple in the salsa if desired.
- Top the nachos with your favorite nacho toppings like black beans, diced tomatoes, and pickled jalapenos.
- Leftover pulled pork can be used in tacos, burritos, or breakfast scrambles.

Nutritional Information
(per serving)

Calories: 700, **Fat**: 40g,
Protein:40g, **Carbs**: 50g

Transform your Blackstone griddle into a smoker for this crowd-pleasing recipe. Tender pulled pork is piled high on a bed of tortilla chips and topped with a refreshing and slightly spicy pineapple salsa for a fiesta in every bite.

BLACKSTONE BEEF BONANZA
GRIDDLE-LICIOUS PERFECTION FOR EVERY CUT

Calling all carnivores! This chapter is your ode to the mighty cow. We're not just talking about throwing a steak on the grill and calling it a day – we're about to unlock the full potential of beef on your trusty Blackstone griddle. From juicy ribeyes to flavorful ground beef, this chapter is a celebration of sizzling perfection for every cut imaginable.

Whether you're a seasoned grill master or a curious grill newbie, we'll guide you through techniques that transform any beef cut into a masterpiece.So, fire up your griddle, grab your favorite cut, and prepare to be amazed! This chapter is your gateway to griddle-licious beef perfection, one delicious recipe at a time. Get ready to explore a world of flavor possibilities and elevate your next beef dish to a whole new level.

Alex & Jamie
Blake

CHEESE-BURGER PERFECTION

SERVES
4

PREP TIME
10 mins

COOK TIME
10 mins

Alex & Jamie
Blake

Here's what you'll need

- 1 pound ground beef (80/20 lean-to-fat ratio)
- 1 tbsp Worcestershire sauce
- 1/2 tsp onion powder
- 1/4 tsp garlic powder
- Salt & pepper to taste
- 4 hamburger buns, toasted
- Your favorite burger toppings (cheese, lettuce, tomato, onion, pickles, etc.)

Let's get griddle-ing!

1. Preheat your griddle to medium-high heat.
2. In a large bowl, gently combine ground beef, Worcestershire sauce, onion powder, garlic powder, salt, and pepper. Don't overmix, as this can make the burgers tough.
3. Form the ground beef mixture into four equal patties.
4. Place the burger patties on the preheated griddle and cook for 3-4 minutes per side, or until desired doneness.
5. While the burgers cook, toast the hamburger buns on the griddle for a minute or two per side.
6. Assemble your burgers with your favorite toppings and enjoy!

Tips

- Use a burger press to create evenly shaped patties.
- Make a thumbprint indentation in the center of each patty to prevent them from puffing up in the middle while cooking.
- Experiment with different cheese varieties like cheddar, Swiss, or blue cheese.
- Leftover burgers can be used in salads, wraps, or sliders.

Nutritional Information
(per serving)

Calories: 450, **Fat**: 30g,
Protein:40g, **Carbs**: 30g

Elevate your burger game with this recipe that delivers juicy, flavorful patties cooked to perfection on your Blackstone griddle.

MONGOLIAN BEEF STIR-FRY

Alex & Jamie
Blake

SERVES
4

PREP TIME
15 mins

COOK TIME
10 mins

Here's what you'll need

- 1 pound flank steak, thinly sliced against the grain
- 1 tbsp cornstarch
- 1 tbsp soy sauce
- 1 tbsp vegetable oil
- 1 red bell pepper, sliced
- 1 green onion, sliced
- Cooked white rice or noodles (for serving)

For the Sauce:
- 1/4 cup low-sodium beef broth
- 1/4 cup soy sauce
- 1 tbsp brown sugar
- 1 tbsp rice vinegar
- 1 tbsp cornstarch
- 1 tsp sriracha (adjust to your spice preference)
- 1 clove garlic, minced
- 1 tsp grated ginger

Let's get griddle-ing!

1. In a bowl, toss the sliced flank steak with cornstarch, soy sauce, and 1 tablespoon of vegetable oil. Let it marinate for at least 15 minutes.
2. In a separate bowl, whisk together all the sauce ingredients.
3. Preheat your griddle to medium-high heat. Add the remaining vegetable oil to the griddle.
4. Working in batches, stir-fry the marinated steak strips for 2-3 minutes per batch, or until browned on the outside. Remove from the griddle and set aside.
5. Add the sliced bell pepper to the griddle and cook for 2-3 minutes, or until softened.
6. Pour the sauce mixture into the griddle and bring to a simmer. Add the cooked steak strips back to the pan and toss to coat them in the sauce.
7. Heat for an additional minute or two, or until the sauce thickens slightly.
8. Serve the Mongolian beef stir-fry over cooked white rice or noodles, garnished with sliced green onions.

Tips

- Substitute flank steak with skirt steak or chicken breast for a different protein option.
- Serve the stir-fry with a side of steamed broccoli or snow peas for added vegetables.
- Leftover stir-fry can be reheated for lunch the next day.

Nutritional Information
(per serving)

Calories: 500, **Fat**: 30g,
Protein:40g, **Carbs**: 40g

This quick and easy stir-fry features tender flank steak strips cooked with a savory and slightly sweet sauce, perfect for a weeknight meal served over rice or noodles.

BACON-WRAPPED FILET MIGNON WITH HERB BUTTER

SERVES
2

PREP TIME
10 mins

COOK TIME
10 mins

Alex & Jamie
Blake

Here's what you'll need

- 2 filet mignon steaks (6-8 oz each)
- 4 slices thick-cut bacon
- Salt & pepper to taste

For the Herb Butter:
- 4 tbsp unsalted butter, softened
- 1 tbsp chopped fresh parsley
- 1 tbsp chopped fresh thyme
- 1 clove garlic, minced
- Salt & pepper to taste

Let's get griddle-ing!

1. Preheat your griddle to medium-high heat.
2. In a small bowl, combine softened butter, chopped parsley, chopped thyme, minced garlic, salt, and pepper to create the herb butter.
3. Season the filet mignon steaks generously with salt and pepper. Wrap each steak with two slices of bacon, securing them with toothpicks if needed.
4. Place the bacon-wrapped filet mignon on the preheated griddle and cook for 4-5 minutes per side for medium-rare, or until desired doneness. An instant-read thermometer can be used to check the internal temperature (145°F for medium-rare).
5. While the steaks cook, melt the remaining herb butter in a small pan on the griddle.
6. Remove the cooked steaks from the griddle and let them rest for a few minutes before slicing.
7. Spoon the herb butter sauce over the sliced steaks and serve immediately.

Tips

- Ask your butcher to cut the filet mignon steaks to your desired thickness.
- Substitute fresh herbs like rosemary or chives for parsley and thyme in the herb butter.
- Leftover steak can be served cold on a bed of salad greens or sliced for sandwiches.

Nutritional Information
(per serving)

Calories: 800, **Fat**: 60g,
Protein:60g, **Carbs**: 5g

Indulge in a luxurious meal with this recipe featuring tender filet mignon steaks wrapped in savory bacon and finished with a creamy herb butter sauce.

BLACKSTONE GRIDDLE TOMAHAWK STEAK

SERVES 1

PREP TIME 10 mins

COOK TIME 15 mins

Alex & Jamie
Blake

Here's what you'll need

- 1 (2-3 pound) tomahawk steak
- 1 tablespoon olive oil
- Salt and freshly ground black pepper
- 1 tablespoon butter (optional)
- Fresh herbs (optional, for garnish)

Let's get griddle-ing!

1. Pat the tomahawk steak dry with paper towels. Season generously with salt and pepper on all sides.
2. Preheat your Blackstone griddle to high heat (around 450°F).
3. Sear the tomahawk steak for 2-3 minutes per side, or until a nice brown crust forms. Searing the edges of the bone is recommended for added flavor.
4. If you prefer a more medium-rare or medium doneness, reduce the heat on one side of the griddle to medium-low (around 300°F). Move the steak to the cooler side and cook for an additional 5-7 minutes per side for medium-rare, or until it reaches your desired internal temperature (see internal temperature guide below).
5. In the last minute of cooking, you can add a tablespoon of butter to the pan and baste the steak with the melted butter for extra flavor.
6. Remove the steak from the griddle and transfer it to a cutting board. Tent with foil and let it rest for 10 minutes to allow the juices to redistribute, resulting in a more tender and flavorful steak.
7. If desired, you can carve the meat off the bone before serving. Slice the steak against the grain for maximum tenderness.
8. Garnish with fresh herbs like rosemary or thyme for a touch of visual appeal.

Tips

- Use a good quality instant-read thermometer to monitor the internal temperature of the steak for perfect doneness.
- A tomahawk steak is a thick cut, so be patient during the cooking process. Don't rush or move the steak too frequently, as this can hinder a good sear.
- If the flame flares up due to the fat dripping from the bone, move the steak to a cooler area of the griddle or reduce the heat slightly.
- Leftover steak can be stored in an airtight container in the refrigerator for up to 3 days or frozen for longer storage.

Nutritional Information (per serving)

Calories: 800, **Fat**: 60g,
Protein:70g, **Carbs**: 0g

This recipe will guide you through searing a juicy and flavorful tomahawk steak, perfect for a special occasion or a satisfying weekend meal.

Internal Temperature Guide:
Rare: 125°F
Medium-Rare: 135°F
Medium: 145°F
Medium-Well: 155°F
Well Done: 160°F

JUICY LUCY BURGERS

SERVES
4

PREP TIME
15 mins

COOK TIME
10 mins

Alex & Jamie
Blake

Nutritional Information (per serving)

Calories: 600, **Fat**: 40g,
Protein:45g, **Carbs**: 35g

This recipe takes your classic cheeseburger to a whole new level by incorporating a gooey cheese center that melts out with every bite.

Here's what you'll need

- 1 pound ground beef (80/20 lean-to-fat ratio)
- 1/2 cup shredded cheddar cheese
- 1 tbsp Worcestershire sauce
- 1/2 tsp onion powder
- 1/4 tsp garlic powder
- Salt & pepper to taste
- 4 hamburger buns, toasted
- Your favorite burger toppings (lettuce, tomato, onion, pickles, etc.)

Let's get griddle-ing!

1. In a large bowl, combine ground beef, Worcestershire sauce, onion powder, garlic powder, salt, and pepper. Don't overmix, as this can make the burgers tough.
2. Divide the ground beef mixture into four equal portions. Form each portion into a patty.
3. Make a deep indentation in the center of each patty. Fill the indentation with shredded cheddar cheese. Pinch the edges of the patty together to seal in the cheese.
4. Preheat your griddle to medium-high heat.
5. Place the stuffed burger patties on the preheated griddle and cook for 3-4 minutes per side, or until desired doneness. Be careful not to press down on the burgers while they cook, as this can squeeze out the cheese filling.
6. Toast the hamburger buns on the griddle for a minute or two per side.
7. Assemble your burgers with your favorite toppings and enjoy the eruption of melted cheese with every bite!

Tips

- Use a burger press to create evenly shaped patties with a deep enough indentation for the cheese.
- Substitute cheddar cheese with your favorite cheese variety like mozzarella, pepper jack, or Swiss cheese.
- Leftover burgers can be used in salads, wraps, or sliders.

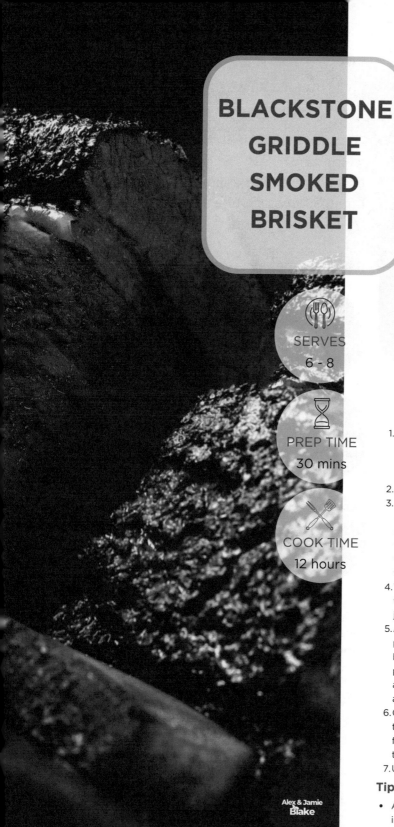

BLACKSTONE GRIDDLE SMOKED BRISKET

SERVES 6 - 8

PREP TIME 30 mins

COOK TIME 12 hours

Alex & Jamie
Blake

Nutritional Information (per serving)

Calories: 450, **Fat:** 30g,
Protein:50g, **Carbs:** 1g

This recipe adapts the traditional low and slow smoking method for brisket to work on a Blackstone griddle. By using a smoke box and adjusting the heat, you can achieve a smoky and flavorful result.

Important Note: This recipe requires monitoring and adding wood chips throughout the cooking process.

Here's what you'll need

- 1 (12-15 pound) packer brisket, trimmed of excess fat
- 2 tablespoons olive oil
- Salt and freshly ground black pepper
- Wood chips for smoking (hickory, oak, or mesquite are good options)
- Optional: Your favorite beef rub

Let's get griddle-ing!

1. Trim any excess fat from the brisket, leaving a thin layer (about 1/4 inch) for flavor. Pat the brisket dry with paper towels. Season generously with salt and pepper on all sides. If using a rub, coat the brisket evenly with your favorite rub.
2. Preheat your Blackstone griddle to medium-low heat (around 225°F).
3. **Smoke Box Setup:** If you have a smoker box attachment for your Blackstone griddle, fill it with wood chips and place it on the preheated griddle. If you don't have a smoker box, you can create a makeshift smoker box by wrapping aluminum foil around a small disposable aluminum pan. Fill the pan with wood chips and poke holes in the foil to allow smoke to escape. Place the pan directly on the griddle near the heat source.
4. You can add a nice sear to the brisket for extra flavor by increasing the heat to medium-high (around 350°F) for a few minutes per side. Sear the brisket just to brown the exterior, then reduce the heat back down to medium-low.
5. Add more wood chips to the smoker box as needed throughout the cooking process, aiming to replenish them every 1-2 hours. Smoke and cook the brisket for 10-12 hours, or until the internal temperature reaches 195°F for pulled brisket or 205°F for sliced brisket. Monitor the brisket regularly and add more wood chips as needed to maintain smoke. You may also need to adjust the griddle heat slightly to maintain the desired temperature range.
6. Once the brisket reaches the desired internal temperature, remove it from the griddle and wrap it tightly in butcher paper or aluminum foil. Let it rest for at least 1-2 hours to allow the juices to redistribute, resulting in a more tender and flavorful brisket.
7. Unwrap the brisket and carve it against the grain into thin slices for serving.

Tips

- A good quality instant-read thermometer is essential for monitoring the internal temperature of the brisket.
- Be patient! Brisket requires a long cook time for optimal tenderness.
- You can add a water pan to the griddle to help regulate temperature and prevent the brisket from drying out. Place the pan on the opposite side of the griddle from the heat source and fill it with about 1 inch of water.
- Leftover brisket can be stored in an airtight container in the refrigerator for up to 3 days or frozen for longer storage.

Safety Note: When using a gas griddle for extended periods, it's important to be attentive and monitor the flame and temperature regularly.

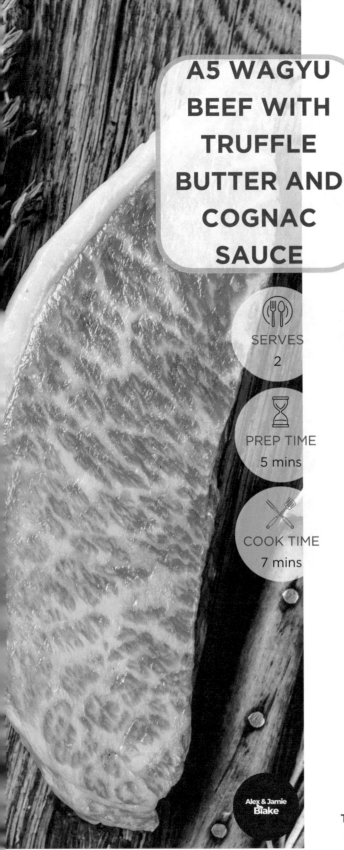

A5 WAGYU BEEF WITH TRUFFLE BUTTER AND COGNAC SAUCE

SERVES
2

PREP TIME
5 mins

COOK TIME
7 mins

Alex & Jamie
Blake

Here's what you'll need

- 2 A5 Wagyu ribeye steaks (6-8 oz each)
- 1 tablespoon high-quality olive oil
- Sea salt flakes and freshly ground black pepper
- 4 tablespoons unsalted butter, softened
- 1 tablespoon black truffle paste (or truffle oil)
- 1/4 cup Cognac
- 1/4 cup beef broth
- 1 tablespoon heavy cream (optional, for a richer sauce)
- Fresh herbs (optional, for garnish): Chopped thyme, rosemary, or parsley

Let's get griddle-ing!

1. Preheat your Blackstone griddle to medium-high heat (around 400°F).
2. Pat the Wagyu steaks dry with paper towels. Season generously with sea salt flakes and freshly ground black pepper on both sides.
3. Drizzle the olive oil on the preheated griddle. Carefully place the Wagyu steaks on the griddle and sear for 1-2 minutes per side for a rare to medium-rare doneness. A5 Wagyu cooks very quickly due to its high fat content, so be careful not to overcook it.
4. While the steaks are searing, prepare the truffle butter. In a small bowl, combine softened butter and black truffle paste (or truffle oil). Mix well to create a flavorful spread.
5. In a separate pan (not on the griddle) heat the Cognac over medium heat until it simmers and reduces slightly. Add the beef broth and bring to a simmer. Scrape up any browned bits from the bottom of the pan. Reduce heat and simmer for a few minutes, or until the sauce thickens slightly. If desired, whisk in the heavy cream for a richer texture. Season with salt and pepper to taste.
6. Remove the Wagyu steaks from the griddle and transfer them to a plate. Top each steak with a generous pat of truffle butter. Let the steaks rest for 5 minutes to allow the juices to redistribute, resulting in a more tender and flavorful experience.
7. Serve the Wagyu steaks immediately, drizzled with any pan drippings from the griddle. Spoon the Cognac sauce alongside the steak, and garnish with fresh herbs (optional).

Tips

- Due to the high cost of A5 Wagyu, it's best to cook it to a rare or medium-rare doneness to truly appreciate its rich flavor and melt-in-your-mouth texture.
- You can substitute regular unsalted butter for the truffle butter if truffle paste or oil is unavailable.
- This recipe is designed to be simple and highlight the quality of the Wagyu beef. You can pair it with simple accompaniments like roasted asparagus, mashed potatoes, or a light salad to avoid overpowering the flavors.

Nutritional Information
(per serving)

Calories: 800, **Fat**: 70g,
Protein:40g, **Carbs**: 5g

This recipe elevates the humble Blackstone griddle to a culinary high note by featuring the luxurious A5 Wagyu beef. The melt-in-your-mouth marbling and rich flavor are further enhanced by a decadent truffle butter and a sophisticated Cognac sauce.

LAMB LOVER'S PARADISE
GRIDDLE-SEARED PERFECTION FOR EVERY CUT

Calling all lamb enthusiasts! This chapter isn't just about chops and shanks – it's a celebration of the versatility and flavor explosion lamb brings to your Blackstone griddle. Imagine perfectly seared lamb chops with a smoky kiss, tender kebabs bursting with vibrant vegetables and spices, or flavorful ground lamb sizzling in flavorful tacos. Craving a showstopper? We've got a recipe for impressive rack of lamb that will leave your guests speechless.

So, fire up your griddle, grab your favorite cut of lamb, and prepare to be amazed! This chapter is your gateway to griddle-licious lamb perfection, one delicious recipe at a time. Get ready to explore a world of flavor possibilities and elevate your next lamb dish to a whole new level.

Alex & Jamie
Blake

SEARED LAMB CHOPS WITH GARLIC HERB BUTTER

SERVES
2

PREP TIME
10 mins

COOK TIME
10 mins

Alex & Jamie
Blake

Here's what you'll need

- 2 bone-in lamb loin chops (6-8 oz each)
- 1 tbsp olive oil
- Salt & pepper to taste

For the Garlic Herb Butter:

- 4 tbsp unsalted butter, softened
- 1 tbsp chopped fresh rosemary
- 1 tbsp chopped fresh thyme
- 1 clove garlic, minced
- Salt & pepper to taste

Let's get griddle-ing!

1. Preheat your griddle to medium-high heat. Pat the lamb chops dry with paper towels. Season generously with olive oil, salt, and pepper.
2. In a small bowl, combine softened butter, chopped rosemary, chopped thyme, minced garlic, salt, and pepper to create the garlic herb butter.
3. Place the seasoned lamb chops on the preheated griddle. Cook for 3-4 minutes per side for medium-rare, or until desired doneness.
4. While the lamb chops cook, melt the garlic herb butter in a small pan on the griddle.
5. Remove the cooked lamb chops from the griddle and let them rest for a few minutes before serving.
6. Spoon the garlic herb butter over the lamb chops and serve immediately.

Tips

- Ask your butcher to French-trim the lamb chops for a cleaner presentation.
- Use a meat thermometer to ensure the internal temperature of the lamb chops reaches 145°F (medium-rare).
- Substitute fresh herbs like parsley or chives for rosemary and thyme in the garlic herb butter.
- Leftover lamb chops can be sliced and used in salads or wraps.

Nutritional Information (per serving)

Calories: 600, **Fat**: 45g,
Protein:50g, **Carbs**: 5g

This classic recipe features perfectly seared lamb chops topped with a decadent garlic herb butter, making for a simple yet elegant main course.

GREEK LAMB BURGERS WITH TZATZIKI SAUCE

SERVES 4

PREP TIME 15 mins

COOK TIME 10 mins

Alex & Jamie
Blake

Here's what you'll need

- 1 pound ground lamb
- 1/4 cup crumbled feta cheese
- 1/4 cup chopped Kalamata olives
- 1 tbsp chopped fresh oregano
- 1/2 tsp dried mint
- 1/4 red onion, finely chopped
- Salt & pepper to taste
- 4 hamburger buns, toasted

For the Tzatziki Sauce:
- 1 cup plain Greek yogurt
- 1/2 cucumber, seeded and grated
- 1 clove garlic, minced
- 1 tbsp olive oil
- 1 tbsp chopped fresh dill
- Salt & pepper to taste

Let's get griddle-ing!

1. In a large bowl, combine ground lamb, crumbled feta cheese, chopped olives, chopped oregano, dried mint, chopped red onion, salt, and pepper. Mix gently to combine.
2. Form the lamb mixture into four equal patties.
3. Preheat your griddle to medium-high heat.
4. Place the lamb burgers on the preheated griddle and cook for 4-5 minutes per side, or until desired doneness.
5. While the burgers cook, prepare the tzatziki sauce by combining Greek yogurt, grated cucumber, minced garlic, olive oil, chopped dill, salt, and pepper in a bowl.
6. Toast the hamburger buns on the griddle for a minute or two per side.
7. Assemble your burgers with your favorite toppings and a generous dollop of tzatziki sauce.

Tips

- Soak the chopped red onion in cold water for 10 minutes to remove some of the harshness.
- Substitute chopped fresh parsley for dill in the tzatziki sauce if desired.
- Leftover lamb burgers can be crumbled and used in salads, lettuce wraps, or pasta dishes.

Nutritional Information (per serving)

Calories: 550, **Fat**: 35g, **Protein**:40g, **Carbs**: 30g

These flavorful lamb burgers infused with classic Greek ingredients like feta cheese, olives, and oregano are a delicious twist on the classic burger.

72

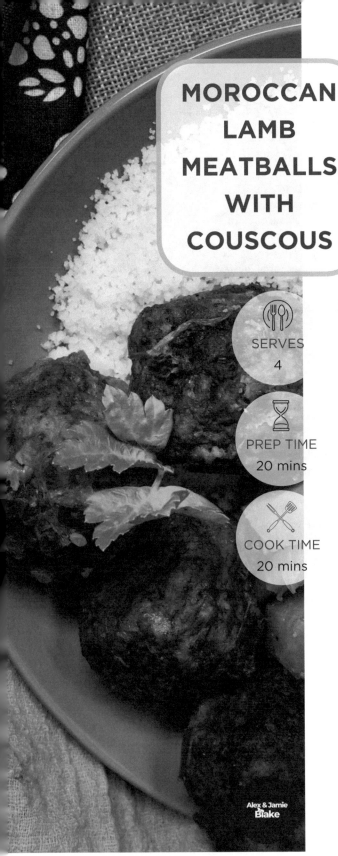

MOROCCAN LAMB MEATBALLS WITH COUSCOUS

SERVES
4

PREP TIME
20 mins

COOK TIME
20 mins

Alex & Jamie
Blake

Nutritional Information
(per serving)
Calories: 500, **Fat**: 25g,
Protein:40g, **Carbs**: 45g

This recipe features succulent lamb meatballs seasoned with Moroccan spices and simmered in a flavorful tomato-based sauce, served over fluffy couscous for a satisfying and exotic meal.

Here's what you'll need

For the Lamb Meatballs:
- 1 pound ground lamb
- 1/2 cup breadcrumbs
- 1/4 cup chopped fresh parsley
- 1 tbsp grated onion
- 1 tsp ground cumin
- 1/2 tsp ground coriander
- 1/4 tsp cinnamon
- 1/4 tsp ground ginger
- Salt & pepper to taste

- 1 tbsp olive oil
- 1 onion, diced
- 2 cloves garlic, minced
- 1 (14.5 oz) can diced tomatoes, undrained
- 1/2 cup chicken broth
- 1/4 cup chopped fresh cilantro
- 2 cups cooked couscous
- Chopped fresh parsley (optional, for garnish)

Let's get griddle-ing!

1. In a large bowl, combine ground lamb, breadcrumbs, chopped parsley, grated onion, cumin, coriander, cinnamon, ginger, salt, and pepper. Mix gently to combine and form into small meatballs (about 1-inch in diameter).
2. Preheat your griddle to medium heat. Heat the olive oil on the griddle.
3. Add the meatballs to the preheated griddle and cook for 5-7 minutes, turning occasionally, until browned on all sides.
4. Remove the browned meatballs from the griddle and set aside.
5. Add the diced onion and minced garlic to the griddle and cook for 2-3 minutes, or until softened.
6. Pour in the diced tomatoes with their juices, chicken broth, and chopped cilantro. Bring to a simmer.
7. Add the browned meatballs back to the sauce and simmer for an additional 10 minutes, or until the meatballs are cooked through and the sauce has thickened slightly.
8. In a separate bowl, prepare the cooked couscous according to package instructions.
9. To serve, spoon the couscous onto plates and top with the Moroccan lamb meatballs and sauce. Garnish with chopped fresh parsley (optional).

Tips
- Substitute ground beef or turkey for the ground lamb if desired.
- Adjust the amount of spices according to your preference for heat.
- Serve the lamb meatballs and sauce with a side of steamed vegetables or pita bread for dipping.
- Leftover meatballs can be used in sandwiches, wraps, or pasta dishes.

GRILLED LAMB KEBABS WITH MINT YOGURT MARINADE

SERVES
4

PREP TIME
30 mins

COOK TIME
10 mins

Alex & Jamie
Blake

Here's what you'll need

- 1 pound boneless, skinless lamb leg, cut into 1-inch cubes
- 1 red bell pepper, cut into chunks
- 1 red onion, cut into wedges
- Wooden skewers (soaked in water for at least 30 minutes to prevent burning)
- Your favorite dipping sauce (tzatziki sauce, chimichurri sauce, etc.)

For the Mint Yogurt Marinade:

- 1 cup plain Greek yogurt
- 1/4 cup chopped fresh mint
- 1 tbsp olive oil
- 1 tbsp lemon juice
- 1 tsp ground cumin
- 1/2 tsp garlic powder
- 1/4 tsp salt
- 1/4 tsp black pepper

Let's get griddle-ing!

1. In a bowl, whisk together Greek yogurt, chopped mint, olive oil, lemon juice, cumin, garlic powder, salt, and pepper to create the mint yogurt marinade.
2. Add the lamb cubes to the marinade and toss to coat evenly. Cover and refrigerate for at least 30 minutes, or up to overnight for deeper flavor.
3. Preheat your griddle to medium-high heat.
4. Thread the marinated lamb cubes, red bell pepper chunks, and red onion wedges onto soaked wooden skewers.
5. Place the skewers on the preheated griddle and cook for 4-5 minutes per side, or until the lamb is cooked through and the vegetables are tender-crisp.
6. Serve the grilled lamb kebabs hot with your favorite dipping sauce (tzatziki sauce, chimichurri sauce, etc.).

Tips

- Use a variety of vegetables for your kebabs, such as zucchini, yellow squash, or cherry tomatoes.
- Marinate the lamb for longer for even more flavorful kebabs.
- Grill the kebabs over indirect heat on your griddle for a gentler cook if desired.
- Leftover grilled lamb can be chopped and used in salads, wraps, or fried rice.

Nutritional Information
(per serving)

Calories: 450, **Fat**: 30g,
Protein:40g, **Carbs**: 20g

These flavorful kebabs feature marinated lamb cubes threaded onto skewers and grilled to perfection on your Blackstone griddle. Serve with your favorite dipping sauce for a fun and interactive meal.

SPICED LAMB GYROS WITH PITA BREAD AND TZATZIKI SAUCE

SERVES
4

PREP TIME
20 mins

COOK TIME
15 mins

Alex & Jamie
Blake

Here's what you'll need

- 1 pound boneless, skinless lamb shoulder, thinly sliced
- 4 pita breads
- For the Tzatziki Sauce (see recipe in Lamb Burgers with Tzatziki Sauce, above)
- Chopped red onion
- Chopped tomato
- crumbled feta cheese (optional)

For the Lamb Marinade:
- 1/2 cup plain Greek yogurt
- 1/4 cup olive oil
- 1 tbsp lemon juice
- 1 tbsp chopped fresh oregano
- 1 tsp dried thyme
- 1/2 tsp ground cumin
- 1/4 tsp garlic powder
- Salt & pepper to taste

Let's get griddle-ing!

1. In a bowl, whisk together Greek yogurt, olive oil, lemon juice, chopped oregano, dried thyme, cumin, garlic powder, salt, and pepper to create the lamb marinade.
2. Add the thinly sliced lamb to the marinade and toss to coat evenly. Cover and refrigerate for at least 30 minutes, or up to overnight for deeper flavor.
3. Preheat your griddle to medium-high heat.
4. Remove the lamb slices from the marinade and shake off any excess.
5. Cook the lamb slices on the preheated griddle for 2-3 minutes per side, or until browned and cooked through.
6. While the lamb cooks, warm the pita breads on the griddle for a minute or two per side.
7. Spread a generous dollop of tzatziki sauce on each warmed pita bread. Top with the cooked lamb slices, chopped red onion, chopped tomato, and crumbled feta cheese (optional).
8. Fold the pita breads to enclose the filling and enjoy!

Tips
- Substitute chicken or beef for the lamb if desired.
- Toast the pita breads on the griddle for a crispier texture.
- Add other toppings to your gyros like chopped cucumber, olives, or hot sauce.
- Leftover lamb slices can be used in salads, wraps, or fried rice dishes.

Nutritional Information
(per serving)

Calories: 500, **Fat**: 30g,
Protein:45g, **Carbs**: 35g

These gyros capture the taste of classic Greek street food with seasoned lamb slices cooked on the griddle and served on warm pita bread with all the fixings.

SEARED LAMB STEAKS WITH ROSEMARY GARLIC BUTTER

SERVES 2

PREP TIME 10 mins

COOK TIME 10 mins

Alex & Jamie Blake

Here's what you'll need

- 2 bone-in lamb loin steaks (1-inch thick)
- 1 tbsp olive oil
- Salt & pepper to taste

For the Rosemary Garlic Butter:

- 4 tbsp unsalted butter, softened
- 2 tbsp chopped fresh rosemary
- 1 clove garlic, minced
- Salt & pepper to taste

Let's get griddle-ing!

1. Preheat your griddle to medium-high heat. Pat the lamb steaks dry with paper towels. Season generously with olive oil, salt, and pepper.
2. In a small bowl, combine softened butter, chopped rosemary, minced garlic, salt, and pepper to create the rosemary garlic butter.
3. Place the seasoned lamb steaks on the preheated griddle. Cook for 4-5 minutes per side for medium-rare, or until desired doneness. Use a meat thermometer to check the internal temperature (145°F for medium-rare).
4. While the lamb steaks cook, melt the rosemary garlic butter in a small pan on the griddle.
5. Remove the cooked lamb steaks from the griddle and let them rest for a few minutes before serving.
6. Spoon the rosemary garlic butter over the lamb steaks and serve immediately.

Tips

- Ask your butcher to French-trim the lamb steaks for a cleaner presentation.
- Sear the lamb steaks for an additional minute per side for a more medium doneness.
- Substitute fresh thyme or parsley for rosemary in the garlic butter.
- Leftover lamb steaks can be sliced thin and served on salads or sandwiches.

Nutritional Information
(per serving)

Calories: 700, **Fat**: 50g,
Protein:60g, **Carbs**: 5g

This recipe features thick-cut lamb steaks cooked to a perfect medium-rare and finished with a decadent rosemary garlic butter sauce.

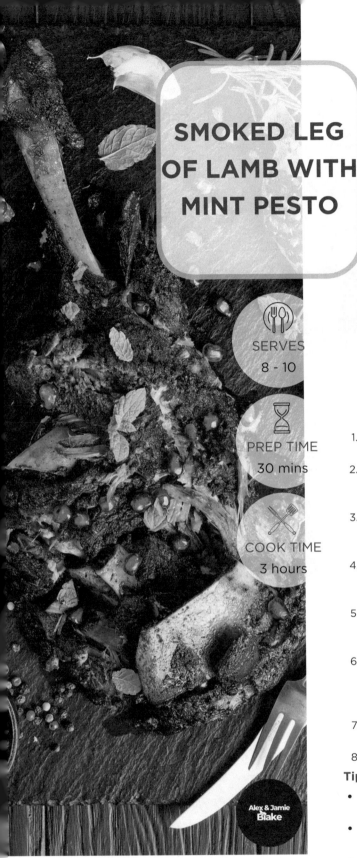

SMOKED LEG OF LAMB WITH MINT PESTO

SERVES
8 - 10

PREP TIME
30 mins

COOK TIME
3 hours

Alex & Jamie
Blake

Here's what you'll need

- 1 bone-in leg of lamb (6-7 pounds)
- 1 tbsp olive oil
- Salt & pepper to taste

For the Mint Pesto:
- 2 cups packed fresh mint leaves
- 1/2 cup grated Parmesan cheese
- 1/4 cup olive oil
- 1/4 cup pine nuts (toasted)
- 2 cloves garlic, minced
- Salt & pepper to taste

For the Smoke Rub:
- 2 tbsp brown sugar
- 1 tbsp paprika
- 1 tbsp chili powder
- 1 tsp garlic powder
- 1 tsp onion powder
- 1/2 tsp smoked paprika
- 1/4 tsp black pepper

Let's get griddle-ing!

1. Preheat your griddle to low (around 225°F) if it has a low setting. If not, use a smoker box filled with wood chips to create smoke.
2. In a small bowl, combine brown sugar, paprika, chili powder, garlic powder, onion powder, smoked paprika, and black pepper to create the smoke rub.
3. Pat the leg of lamb dry with paper towels. Season generously with olive oil, salt, and pepper. Apply the smoke rub evenly over the entire surface of the lamb.
4. Place the seasoned leg of lamb on the preheated griddle. If using a smoker box, add wood chips according to the manufacturer's instructions.
5. Smoke the lamb for 2-3 hours, or until the internal temperature reaches 160°F (medium-rare). You may need to add additional wood chips periodically to maintain smoke.
6. While the lamb smokes, prepare the mint pesto by combining fresh mint leaves, grated Parmesan cheese, olive oil, toasted pine nuts, and minced garlic in a food processor. Process until a smooth paste forms. Season with salt and pepper to taste.
7. Once cooked, remove the leg of lamb from the griddle and let it rest for at least 30 minutes before carving.
8. Carve the lamb and serve with the prepared mint pesto.

Tips

- Use a meat thermometer to ensure the internal temperature of the lamb reaches 160°F (medium-rare) for the most tender results.
- Wrap the cooked leg of lamb in butcher paper or aluminum foil for an additional 30 minutes to an hour for even more tender meat.
- Leftover lamb can be used in salads, sandwiches, or quesadillas. The mint pesto can also be used as a spread for sandwiches or a topping for pasta dishes.

Nutritional Information
(per serving)

Calories: 500, **Fat**: 35g,
Protein:55g, **Carbs**: 5g

This recipe transforms your Blackstone griddle into a smoker, creating a tender and flavorful whole leg of lamb infused with smoky goodness and topped with a refreshing mint pesto.

Conquering the Kitchen: Essential Conversion Charts & Equivalents

In the culinary world, precision plays a vital role. The perfect balance of ingredients is what separates a delightful dish from a culinary disaster. But recipe measurements can sometimes feel like a foreign language, with cups, ounces, grams, and milliliters swirling in a confusing dance. Fear not, fellow food enthusiasts! This chapter equips you with essential conversion charts and equivalents, transforming you into a measurement maestro in the kitchen.

Conversion Charts: Your Culinary Compass

Imagine a world where you can effortlessly convert between cups of flour and grams of sugar, or seamlessly switch between Fahrenheit and Celsius for baking temperatures. This chapter equips you with three key conversion charts to navigate recipe measurements with confidence:

- Volume Conversions: This chart tackles the common battle between cups and milliliters (ml), ounces (oz), and fluid ounces (fl oz). It allows you to convert wet and dry ingredients with ease, ensuring you never end up with a soup instead of a cake batter.

Measurement	Equivalent in Milliliters (ml)	Equivalent in Ounces (oz)	Equivalent in Fluid Ounces (fl oz)
1 cup	240 ml	8 oz	8 fl oz
½ cup	120 ml	4 oz	4 fl oz
¼ cup	60 ml	2 oz	2 fl oz
1 tablespoon (Tbsp)	15 ml	½ oz	½ fl oz
1 teaspoon (tsp)	5 ml	¼ oz	¼ fl oz

- Weight Conversions: This chart focuses on grams (g) and ounces (oz), allowing you to precisely measure dry ingredients like flour, sugar, and spices. No more overflowing measuring spoons or under-filled baking pans!

Measurement	Equivalent in Grams (g)	Equivalent in Ounces (oz)
1 pound (lb)	454 g	16 oz
½ pound (lb)	227 g	8 oz
¼ pound (lb)	113 g	4 oz
1 cup all-purpose flour	120 g	4.2 oz
1 cup granulated sugar	200 g	7.1 oz
1 cup brown sugar, packed	220 g	7.8 oz

- Temperature Conversions: This chart bridges the gap between Fahrenheit (°F) and Celsius (°C), crucial for baking and cooking where temperature control is essential. No more scrambling to convert oven temperatures or wondering if the water is hot enough for boiling pasta.

Temperature (°F)	Equivalent in Celsius (°C)
350 °F	175 °C
375 °F	190 °C
400 °F	200 °C
425 °F	220 °C
450 °F	230 °C

Conclusion: The Griddle Lifestyle Awaits

As you've journeyed through this exploration of Blackstone Griddle recipes, you've undoubtedly discovered the incredible versatility this griddle offers. It's more than just a grill; it's a transformative outdoor cooking experience. From searing steaks to simmering sauces, from delicate seafood to fluffy pancakes, the Blackstone Griddle empowers you to create a vast array of culinary delights.

The Benefits of the Griddle Lifestyle

- **Effortless Cooking**: The Blackstone Griddle's large, flat surface makes cooking a breeze. No more struggling to flip delicate foods or maneuvering over uneven grates.
- **Versatility Unbound**: This griddle isn't confined to just grilling. It can sear, stir-fry, saute, simmer, and even bake! The possibilities are endless.
- **Quick and Even Heating**: The griddle's smooth surface heats up quickly and distributes heat evenly, ensuring consistent cooking results.
- **Easy Cleanup**: The smooth, non-stick surface makes cleaning a breeze. Simply wipe down the griddle with hot water and a spatula after cooking.
- **Entertainment Central**: The Blackstone Griddle becomes the center of attention at any gathering. Friends and family will flock around as you whip up delicious meals and create lasting memories.

Final Thoughts: A Culinary Canvas for Unforgettable Memories

he Blackstone Griddle is more than just a cooking appliance; it's a gateway to a richer outdoor culinary experience. It's a canvas for your creativity, allowing you to explore new flavors and techniques. It's a facilitator of connection, bringing people together around the shared joy of good food.

Imagine yourself sizzling fajitas for a lively fiesta, flipping fluffy pancakes for a delightful weekend breakfast, or charring vegetables for a healthy and flavorful side dish. The Blackstone Griddle fuels these moments and countless others, transforming your backyard into a stage for culinary adventures and unforgettable memories.

Join the Blackstone Griddle Community

Don't embark on this griddle journey alone! The Blackstone community is a vibrant hub of inspiration and support. Here you'll find a wealth of recipes, tips, and techniques to elevate your griddle skills. Connect with fellow Blackstone enthusiasts, share your creations, and be inspired by their culinary adventures.

Here are some ways to join the Blackstone Griddle community

- Visit the Blackstone Griddle website for a how-to guides, and inspirational content.
- Follow Blackstone Griddle on social media for daily recipe inspiration, cooking tips, and a glimpse into the lives of other griddle enthusiasts.
- Connect with Blackstone Griddle groups and forums online to share your experiences, ask questions, and learn from others.

With your Blackstone Griddle and the support of the vibrant community, you're well on your way to unlocking a world of culinary possibilities and creating memories that will last a lifetime. So fire up your griddle, embrace the griddle lifestyle, and get ready to experience the joy of outdoor cooking at its finest!

Made in the USA
Columbia, SC
16 July 2024

38729173R00046